EVOLVING | **CRANE**

VSN | 3

Book One | Evolving Crane

Dave Temperance Welch

Evolving Crane

Registration Number: VAu001086574

Written by Dave Temperance Welch

Edited by Jim Spivey, Natalie Leffall, Dr. Holland, and Erin Bledsoe

Final Reading by Megan Raymond

Cover Art by Ryan Schwarz

Table of Contents

Dedication......6

Prologue......8

CHAPTER: 1

The first Assault......9

CHAPTER: 2

Your move......23

CHAPTER: 3

Recalling the Past | Canieya......30

CHAPTER: 4

Recalling the Past | Crane......38

CHAPTER: 5

Upturn

Part 1......52

CHAPTER: 6

Student of the Month......62

CHAPTER: 7

The Dunlos......71

CHAPTER: 8

Upturn

Part 2.........95

CHAPTER: 9

MI-6.........100

CHAPTER: 10

Game Day.........108

CHAPTER: 11

The Poof!.........119

CHAPTER: 12

Gateways.........137

CHAPTER: 13

Fine!.........175

CHAPTER: 14

Disclosure.........187

CHAPTER: 15

The Hit List.........195

CHAPTER: 16

Wraith

Part 1 207

CHAPTER: 17

A Wave Goodbye 229

CHAPTER: 18

Cliff Jumping 234

CHAPTER: 19

When Clocks Elapse 238

CHAPTER: 20

The Hall Drag 247

CHAPTER: 21

Change of Plans 258

CHAPTER: 22

The Fact Matter Room 263

CHAPTER: 23

Time Buckle Thesis 268

CHAPTER: 24

Blood Space 275

CHAPTER: 25

Gastropoda: Gray Garden..284

Thank You..299

Acknowledgments 301

excerpt_ A

Evolving | **Crane**

Book 2|Archipus

Dedication

For Levi, my first born.

"I am more than a god, for he cannot harm you with his hands."

7-Dial

Prologue

Behind constellations, too distant to fathom, lies a rock about the size of several solar systems. This asteroid is known as the Layo Galaxy—the mother of all gravity.

Here, the Xaris, a humanoid nation of programs, conflict with a race of slugs. Ever since time's conception, the phylum has limited the automatons' quest.

Because of this, the living programs formed a coalition known as the Symbassy. And without ambivalence, the political body resorted to genocidal amplifications, nearly rendering the slug species extinct.

At last, swaying the format of existence, the Xaris established supremacy over the galaxy, and the master race of androids ruled the day.

Until…

Today.

CHAPTER: 1

The first Assault

|SaMeits Cycle ^{xncz} | (transl) August 5, 2025
Layo Galaxy, Upper Riaxon: Grand Valla

Guffaws from this sacred gathering filled the luxurious hall. And the Feuler was to blame.

The laughter subsided with a turbo speed, as Pias, President of Zenadale, scolded, "And then you *ate* them? Feuler, your mental illness has cost this operation dearly. Eliza!" He shouted.

"Yes sir." The APA responded.

"Reiterate the purpose of Space Void for our Feuler."

"Space Void is a sacred caucus held every cycle by the most renowned officials of the galaxy. Our purpose is to own the universe and everything in between. This caucus insures it. Now that our operation has reached ninety percent, the Symbassy is in route to acquire Earth. Our Feuler…" She hesitated. "…was appointed for schematic retrieval. After Space Lot: Alpha's integration, Horace Vaydin could deploy dozens of gateways over the Earth. Commandeering would begin as soon as next cyc-"

"Yadda. Yadda. Yadda" Pias interrupted. "And then, you *ate* the schematics?"

"Nope! Yes he did." The Feuler answered.

"Wait," whispered Fice, Symbassy Coordinator. "Let me get this straight. Kontriss, and his drug peddling, is tainting

Symbassy trade. The Flavius, and their secretions are polluting the aura. And we can't acquire Earth because the Feuler *ate* our gateway diagrams? Those schematics should've been a digital upload. So did you eat the physical diagrams or the drive containing them?"

"Yes," the Feuler answered.

The crowd muttered while Fice shook his head, rattling his topaz dreads. "You've got to be the **stupidest** spy I've ever encountered!"

"Stupid? He just called you stupid," the Feuler muttered. "He sure did. Cause he definitely wasn't talking to me."

Pias growled as the Feuler continued to speak in mindless circles.

The Feuler raised his hand. Then he grabbed it and slammed it to the table.

Baf!

"We'd like to apologize," the Feuler answered with a rugged voice.

"We?" asked Straton, head of Dimensional Transit.

"He's hoping to shine some light on this discussion. No, I'm not." the Feuler blurted.

A streak of unease shot through the room as the delegates stared at the Feuler.

He was covered in a dark gray cloak of uneven fabric. It appeared to be dense and weighty, with multiple layers that didn't crease. The hood was larger than usual and hid much of his face.

In fact, the Feuler's face was a mystery unto itself. The more you gazed at it, the more you strayed into a chasm created by its confounding outline. But then, his stimulating eyes glowed bright with a heat that spread out from the hooded cloak.

"Now. Where were we…?" the Feuler whispered as he placed his hands on the cybernetic table.

"Huh?" The Feuler reacted as if someone had spoken, then he rambled on. "We have a lot of information to share. No, you don't. You're always lying."

"This guy is off…" inserted Kuzar, Quadrant Divisor.

"Feuler." Pias held out his hand, gesturing for the documents. "Do you have the diagrams, or not?"

The Feuler looked to the ceiling with his guiltless eyes of damnation. "…I looked at those diagrams right before you ate them." He then shouted, "**You** ate them! I didn't eat them. Yes, you did! I was standing right beside you. I witnessed it."

"Okay… Feuler?" Pias asked.

"Well…maybe I did," the Feuler hissed.

"Feuler!" screamed Pias. "Who are you talking to?"

"Well now…" said the Feuler. "That depends on who *you're* talking to." The delegates whispered amongst themselves as the Feuler grumbled with a scowl. "Me… Or me…"

The report of a weapon echoed throughout the chamber, turning every head in the infamous rally.

The Feuler stared into the snub barrel of Pias's Verne Gat, a dark matter disruptor.

"Sir?" Eliza blurted. As she backed away, the Feuler slouched in his seat.

Suddenly… a colossal knife chopped through Pias's wrist.

CHkp!

"AAAAgaaaaaggghhhhh!" Pias screamed. He grabbed his bloody nub as the Vern Gat shattered. His severed hand wobbled to the floor.

The Feuler yanked his knife from the table and—

—Klop!

The blade wedged into Pias's mouth, splitting his jawbone.

Blood splattered across the table, splashing in several faces.

"AAaahhhhhhhhh!" Eliza screamed as Pias stood, toppling his chair to the floor.

"Shut up!" the Feuler bleated.

He cut off Pias's other hand and then his right leg. He sliced clean through Pias's abdomen, whisking off his forearm.

The Feuler's cloak sat in his seat like a malignant disease as the officials gathered their wits. Suddenly, the garment jacked into the ceiling and the meeting went bonkers.

The Feuler chopped off Pias's other forearm and his shoulders. While standing behind Pias, the Feuler reached over and thrust the knife into Pias's chest.

Shuc!

He ripped Pias open, slopping his intestines onto the table. They sloshed to the floor.

The delegates sprinted for the door as the Fueler diced through Pias's head, hacking off his scalp. It twisted across the room, bumping against the far wall.

Bift!

Eliza screeched to a halt as the Feuler popped up and chopped into her skull.

Bash!

A gory current spilled over the room as her arm flailed through the air. She toppled to the ground.

The leaders stumbled into one another, slipping in Eliza's blood. It was then when they noticed: The Feuler was of slug descent—the exact same race they had been attempting to eradicate.

This variant, this disgusting and deformed creature, was nothing like they imagined. The sight of the Feuler, in this light, was awfully sickening and paralyzing.

His skin was gray with a hint of green and profusely sweaty, slimy, gleamy, and full of colorful spots and speckles. He was scrawny and lengthy, yet full of boulder-like muscles. The Feuler (also a butcher by trade) wore thick, beige, knee-length cargo shorts, frayed at the ends and a matching chunky utility belt supported his shorts. But the Feuler was anatomically correct, barefooted, and immensely fast. And shockingly enough, this butcher had somehow split in half. Right. Down. The middle.

The Feuler's left half and the Feuler's right half—FL and FR—were twins born of the same demonic force.

Because of this division, the Feuler's coordination narrowed to minor hops and leaps. His organs were exposed between the openings of the two halves. The various innards operated in harmonious agreement but on their own impulses. They seemed to be held in place by a thick, impenetrable sac of gelatin, fastened to the edges of each unique half. Several clasps flowed through the median of the Feuler's hideous body. They may have been used to keep the gelatin sac in place.

The delegates scrambled to the middle of the room.

Communicating with a pair of hair-thin antennae, FR slid in front of the entry door while FL stood between the table and the window.

FR darted into the crowd, cutting off Straton's face.

Straton hit the floor.

Ordis, The Governor of Riaxon, ran for the door, but FR spun around and diced off his hand.

Zssch!

"YYYYeaaaaahhhheee!" he screamed as a senator bumped into the meeting table. FL slid on top of the table, tossing his knife into the air. He kicked the senator in the face with a backflip.

Crak!

The senator's head whiplashed to the table.

FL caught the knife, and swiped—

Thohpp!

The senator's head thudded against the wall.

Pawf!

Gore gushed from the senator's neck. As his body slid off the table, Vice President, Cronz, glared in fear.

Bleeding from the wrist, Ordis turned to open the main door, but FR was sticking to the wall behind him.

FR clutched the knife in his mouth, and snatched Ordis by the collar, slamming his back to the door.

FR spat the knife from mouth to hand. He stabbed into Ordis's stomach and raked at an angle.

"AAAgghhhh!" Ordis screamed as his chest ruptured.

Cronz bolted for the door. But FL gripped his knife by the mouth and snatched him back.

"Eugk!" Cronz shouted as FL slammed him into the table.

Stabbing into his pelvis, FL slit through Cronz like a piece of worn silk.

"EEEEAaaaaggghhh!" Cronz yelled as his flesh unzipped.

Near the entry door, FR chopped into Fice's chest, forcing him back into the table.

As FL cut through Cronz with a circular swipe, his knife plunged into Fice's head.

Bish!

Blood gushed from the combined attack.

FL snatched his blade from Fice's head while FR yanked his knife from Fice's chest. Their antennae twitched as Fice slumped to the floor.

FR backed up to the door while FL slid from the table.

The stench of death filled the air, and the once-chuckling crowd of senators had been reduced to a sea of milky blood. At the helm of this massacre was the Feuler. The knife-wielding butcher had yet to realize, anything…

Kuzar and Riva eyed the room's entrance, but FR stood in front of the door.

Kuzar took refuge under the large cybernetic table.

Riva glanced over the room, searching for the Feuler's other half. As he backed into the table, he spun around wildly, assuming the table was FL.

Riva giggled in fear as he climbed on top of the table.

FR slid from the door and to the end of the table. While gripping his knife's handle with determination, his antenna twitched with subtlety.

Riva glanced to the door, as FL mounted the table.

Bakt!

He chopped into the delegate's head as FR launched onto the table, hacking into Riva's groin.

Shussssk!

As FR cut up, FL cut down, slicing Riva in two. The blades melted through the official so fast that Riva never left the table.

To the Feuler, this was a splendid slice of refinement, but this horrible butcher's "masterpiece" was quite distasteful to the eye.

Unlike the Feuler, Riva didn't have a gelatin sac to house

his innards. His halved body slid to the blood-swamped floor. The visceral entrails oozed out of his skin's casing, scattering in erratic directions, adding **gore** to the disorder.

Splat!

The blood-soaked bowels landed in front of Kuzar. He cringed under the table, grabbing his mouth.

Suddenly, the Feuler snatched Kuzar from under the table.

The delegate slipped. His face smacked the floor.

Wakt!

He jumped to his feet and sprinted for the door, reaching as if it were in arm's length. With so much adrenaline rushing through his body, he didn't feel his hand as it flew off.

Bouncing against the entry door, the severed hand soared over his head and whipped back under the table. Kuzar gawked at his sizzling hand.

Suddenly, his arm fell off.

Fwzzzzzzz!

Blood danced about the official's face as he stared at his fallen limb. "NNNooooo…," he mumbled.

Kuzar turned to the entry door, but FR stood in his face.

FL approached Kuzar from behind, juggling his knife in

the air. Then, both halves attacked the delegate.

Streaks of blood-spurting incisions sliced Kuzar into deli meat.

FL and FR came to a still as Kuzar attempted to speak. But the official dispersed into a thousand scanty segments.

The shavings fell with exquisite precision, and for several moments, did they flake into a pile of useless remains.

The butcher observed with diligence, ensuring that each sliver fell in its appropriate spot. Such a gory carnage of art that only the Feuler could provide.

"Fetching…," FR mumbled.

FL turned toward FR and their clasps reacted like solenoids, aligning the halves in tandem. The Feuler's body locked back together with clicks, and clacks.

He sheathed his massive, bloody butcher knives into the holsters on the rear of his belt.

His menacing cloak hung in the corner of the desecrated hall. The huge garment traveled over to the Feuler. Descending from the air, it covered the psychopathic butcher underneath.

Shrouded in such mystery, the glowy-eyed Feuler exited the sacred hall.

As the doors to Space Void closed, the stomach-churning sight, fizzed in a repulsive stew.

CHAPTER: 2

Your move

Layo Galaxy, Upper Riaxon: The Outskirts

Suns of bliss shone with rigid moonlets and clashing planets filling the distant skies. The Unitran bolted across the air at quantum speeds, coasting smoothly over the hyper rails. Celestial rings hovered to a still, smothering the inverted setting. Aliens stirred with galactic travel in aerial pods and shuttles while an old clunky spacecraft zapped through the bustling traffic.

This dingy brown and dented oval craft had two massive engines structured into the sides of its ovel design. The craft flew with urgency as it settled abruptly about Grand Valla's landing pad.

Neriya, of Xarnan, better known as Meth, is of slug decent, a Symbassy spy, and apparently late- due to her faulty lines of communication. But needless to say, the gorgeous mollusk had finally arrived.

Meth trekked briskly across the landing pad.

Eut! Eut! - her TPD sounded. She took the device from her pocket and typed briefly into the transparent monitor. As Meth entered Grand Valla the Feuler exited Grand Valla- *incognito* in fashion.

Meth rushed into the lobby barefooted, tucking her TPD away while glancing over the immaculate setting. Her flaunting presence mesmerized the Xaris officials, turning every head in the room.

She stood about five feet and some change. Her skin was gray and green, with flattering black and blue spots running down her back, arms, and legs. She wore a pair of compression shorts and a half-sleeve coat, cropped above her waist. But her dynamic body and attire conflicted with her overall mission.

Burdened enough by her tardy arrival, the sensible workers came to a stall. Because every delegate of Space Void was still in attendance. And no one had the nerve to question Meth's tardy arrival.

Standing behind the concierge's desk was Thorice Senitel, the head of Grand Valla's management team. He wore a dashing all-black suit, tailored and styled with a black shirt and necktie to match. He was a bit older and more than mindful of his commitment to Grand Valla.

"Greetings, how can we assist you?" Thorice asked.

Meth stared with a set of captivating eyes while Thorice waited patiently for a response.

A fellow employee with a handful of papers walked by and slowed to a stop. "Hey! You're...," he mumbled.

Meth stomped over to the employee. He was of Inatech descent and still among the younger crowd.

"You're one of Ruckus' students at the school for combat tennis," the employee exclaimed. "What's the name... Kontiemar? That's one brutal form of self-defense."

"I'm here for Pias," Meth responded.

Thorice replied sincerely, "I'm sorry, ma'am. He's in a me—"

"I can see that," Meth interrupted. "Their vehicles are still outside."

"I'm sure they will be more than happy that you have arrived," Thorice explained while Meth, agitated by his response, turned to the Teledeck in the corner of the lobby.

"Bail," Thorice shouted.

"Yes sir!" Bail jumped to attention.

"Would you mind escorting her up?"

"Yes sir!"

Just then, everything stopped.

Thorice glared over to the main entry door.

Bail gazed in the same direction and stumbled, dropping his documents to the floor.

PLftt!!

"I—I'm sorry," he stuttered as he grabbed up his things.

Meth finally looked over her shoulder and at this same uncomfortable image.

"As I live and breathe… Meth, my dear," grumbled a dark and monstrous voice.

A look of fear nested in the faces of Thorice and the officials. However, Meth, with her galvanizing presence, was just as formidable as the dreaded Simma Fice—brother to Velleyan Fice.

Simma stood tall with smooth pink skin. His red hair spiked with an array of dreads. He had a black cloth tied about his face with a faded red X in the center. He wore dirty brown gloves, a tattered blue jacket, a black T-shirt, black-and-white striped pants, and black boots. His eyes were bloodshot red, as he had no pupils.

His arrival was so revolting because, to the simple-minded, Simma's extremely hazardous.

Simma Fice, also known as Chest Pain, had a dangerous but unique gift. He was born with the ability to control and summon organs from the cavity of another being, living or deceased.

He gazed deep into Meth's eyes, waiting for her to reply, but Meth only searched for words that she couldn't find.

"I was told the meeting would only last a moment," said Simma while turning to face Thorice.

"Ya-yes, sir. He and the others are still meeting," Thorice replied with a trembling voice.

"I—I was just about to show Mrs.… I'm sorry, ma'am. I didn't get your name," inserted Bail.

Meth glared into Bail's eyes. "Take me there. Now!"

"Yes ma'am," Bail replied.

Milky Way Galaxy | Space Lot: Alpha

Hundreds of miles from the Earth's moon, a massive base floated among the stars. On this base was several spacecrafts and a technologically advanced lab. This facility came with a blue hue illuminating its setting. A huge keyboard stretched from wall to wall, which operated an even larger master computer. Then, a massive monitor hung from the ceiling. At the helm of this screen sat a man… a corrupt, blood-thirsty, super brain criminal.

Diinng! - a message chimed.

The super brain culprit peered up to the screen, after receiving a message from the Layo Galaxy. He translated the Layian dialect.

'Expediting planetarian mobilization. Upload schematics for Gateway integration.'

The mastermind typed away. While the information uploaded, the wicked man sat back into his rolling chair.

Diinng! -the memo sounded.

With a devilish smirk, he translated the Layian dialect.

'TPD's paired for Earth Arm affiliate. Your move…'

As the cursor in the massive monitor pulsed with a relaxing spell, time slipped into an odd pair of achy memories.

CHAPTER: 3

Recalling the Past | Canieya

***

November 18, 2014
New York, New York

Crane?

Whew! Guy's *kinda* hard to forget… Like the day he drove his car *forward*, but in reverse down the middle of Fifth Avenue.

He was not your typical male; I'll tell you that much…

Crane was black. Nah… Blacker than that. Yea. That's about right. He was six-foot-two, rugged and built with a ripped physique. He kept a well-groomed low haircut, and stubbly facial hair. His eyes where small and brown. His nose was big, and his distinct jawline and cheekbones bulged from his sharp face.

He used to stand in the kitchen and eat. It was strange because he would stare right into my eyes the whole time. And I could only gaze at him for so long before I would blush from the chemistry between us.

He wasn't too wordy. Yet I wanted so much more out of him. Not just the sex (which was outstanding), but I wanted to know why he did the things he did.

Crane was violent. But he never hit me. Not even once.

He used to pop up at my house covered in blood. And I never figured out how he got in; he didn't have a key. But me, having been the woman—no, the *caring* woman that I was (and I do emphasize *was*), I wouldn't ask any questions. I'd just scour him down with a pressure washer or whatever I could get my hands on.

Sometimes it would take me a few minutes to put two and two together. Other times I'd get all my answers from the evening news, and occasionally right before he would show up.

Then there were moments when I would get so engulfed in Crane's secrets I would fear for his safety. But my house was the safest place for him; no one expected me to harbor a known fugitive.

Crane and I met a long time ago. I was still completing my master's in criminal justice at the time. And after twenty-one weeks in Quantico, Virginia, I returned to New York City. And that's when I met Crane—at a bank robbery.

Our unit pulled up outside the building around 1:00 a.m. I was ordered to stay behind and observe while the senior agents circled the bank, swiveling their flashlights.

A shadow sprinted through the parking lot as I opened the car. While homing in on the silhouette, I lost the figure in the shadows. Just as I stood to aid my search, a man popped up beside me. As I recovered from his startling appearance, the man handed me a note and he ducked off into the alley.

This happened so fast I didn't call it in.

Looking down at the wadded-up paper, I opened it slowly to see his phone number.

Well, I called him of course. Maybe I was trying to capture him or maybe find his accomplice. That worked well…

Over time, I developed more confidence in Crane. He even trained me in several forms of combat.

He was a second-degree black belt in jujitsu and aikido, and a third-degree black belt in Tae kwon do. He was also quite versed in kickboxing, boxing, and wrestling.

One day he said to me, "Candy, I'm going to show you how to fuck somebody up."

But I already knew how to fight, just not like him.

"Okay!" I said, and just like that, my training began. For five years straight, Crane trained me in my backyard. And every day, I was inconceivably subjected to his arduous teachings and myriad drills. He even taught me how to shoot a gun with a higher level of precision.

He told me, "Candy, I've been in hundreds of fights and dozens of shoot outs. But I've never killed a man a day in my life, but you…You, however, are something else. I can see the killer in your eyes. You have a tremendous amount of vigor. It's a toughness about you that amazes me."

Crane sat cross-legged in front of me, about a few feet away. He continued softly. "You don't process pain the same way as the average man, or any human for that matter."

He thought I was an alien.

Crane didn't crack a smile as I laughed.

"You don't believe in aliens?" he asked.

"Um… no," I replied. "Well, I don't know. The probability of them coming to Earth is highly unlikely."

He looked up into the sun without blinking and mumbled, "Canieya, you must be ready for anything and everything. The universe expands in great detail, and we as humans have yet to uncover our truest level of intellect."

Just then, my life flashed before my eyes.

He swung at me so hard he knocked the wind out of me.

With a grunt, I guarded the attack, gasping for air.

He yelled, "Hold your breath!" but continued to attack me from the ground.

He kicked, and I defended.

Then he squatted even lower to the earth and lunged his entire body at me, tackling me to the ground. He landed on top of me with his knee digging into my chest. The pressure was immense.

"Breathe in through your nose!!" he shouted.

That gave me enough strength to ward off his barrage.

"Shrimp! Shrimp!!" He screamed.

I wrapped my feet around his rear leg to lock it in place. Then I (shrimped) scooted my hips back, and I grabbed his knee and shoved him off my chest. A wisp of air entered my lungs.

"Good!" he said.

Grabbing his shoulder, I swung my leg around his waist, and mounted his back. Next, I applied a guillotine choke from the rear. But before I could solidify the position, he quickly slipped out of my grasp. It was as if he had anticipated the move.

Our shuffling on the ground ended with us on our knees.

I whirled around to face him, only to stare deep into the barrel of a gun. "Crane?"

"You're hesitating, Lawson," he replied.

Slapping my hands around the gun and his wrist, I released the firearm from his grip and caught the weapon before it hit the ground.

Scuffling to my feet, I shook out of control.

This fiasco was over.

While cautiously backing away, I kept the gun aimed directly at his head. Did I really know this man?

Staring down to the ground, he mumbled under his breath, "Pull the trigger."

"Pull the trigger!" He shouted as I stood speechless and shaking.

Never in our years of training had Crane ever attacked me like this. It was too real…

"If you don't pull the trigger, Lawson, I am going to kill you," Crane snarled, glaring at me with a twisted smile. "To be honest with you, I hate cops," he continued in a devilish tone.

By then, I was starting to regain focus. My heart settled, although I felt it breaking.

"Do it, Lawson!" he yelled.

All I wanted to say was, "I love you," but the tears flowed down my face, and I dared to wipe them. My nose started running as I sobbed through this mess.

"Your heart is your failure. And because of that, I'm going to kill you...weakling," he uttered.

He stood slowly, but I put enough distance between us to see his every move.

"Don't do it, Crane," I demanded as he stood. "Crane!"

He looked into my eyes with a deadly, cavernous gaze that utterly perplexed me.

I pulled the trigger…

CHAPTER: 4

Recalling the Past | Crane

November 18, 2014
New York, New York

Canieya been crazy!

I'm speaking from my own perspective here.

Chicks don't ever tell the whole story.

Of course, I took the bullets out of my gun.

Do you honestly think I would give Canieya a loaded weapon? I'm crazy, but I ain't *that* crazy. Shiiddd, for a minute there, I saw *my* life flash before *my* eyes.

After she pulled the trigger, I started laughing. She looked down at the gun as if it had malfunctioned. With my hand out, I smiled while approaching her with caution.

She pulled the trigger again and again.

"You jackass!" she shouted before she pitched the gun at me like a baseball.

"You fuck!" she blurted as I caught the firearm.

"Okay. Lawson… I was just kidding," I hollered as she stormed off to the house. "I needed to know! … Baybayyyy!!"

She kept going, slamming the door behind her as I followed.

Must've struck a nerve. Maybe I took her training a bit too

far. But as I opened the back door, I called with concern, "Cani"

—*Crash!*

A vase hurtled into the wall as I ducked behind a couch screaming, "What the fuck!?"

"You took my trust, and you tore it to shreds!" she screamed. "I could stab the living shit out of you right now."

While squatting behind the couch, I put my hands in the air and hollered, "Yield! Yield! I'm sorry, baby! I needed to know you were ready."

"Stay the fuck away from me!" She stomped through the house and kicked into the bedroom.

"Baybay!" I shouted, but she responded with a bunch of commotion. "Canniiieyyyaaa!"

"Fuck you!" she retorted.

My head lifted slowly from behind the couch.

The coast was clear.

As I walked carefully to the bedroom, she blustered in such ill-bred displeasure. "Should've had you arrested a long time ago. You are my enemy, Crane. You tried to kill me. You threatened a police officer!"

"Yeah, but you're still alive, and… you still love me."

"It's overrated."

"Are you bleeding, Canieya? Did I break any of your bones?"

"That's not the point, fuckface!"

With my back still against the wall, I approached the edge of the bedroom doorway. "I wouldn't dare hurt you."

"Shittin' me!" she blurted. "I'm so pissed right now. This or that, what just happened, or what's still happening… It's too real. I'm convinced!"

"Okay, that bit with the gun was too far… I'm sorry…" I whispered as I entered the room and caught a glimpse of her packing.

"Alright!" I spoke. "I'll let you take me in…Straight up. Just don't leave."

The pace of her packing slowed. Then I heard her mumbling something with her back still turned. But I couldn't understand what she was saying, because I was too caught up gazing at her ass. Damn, I wanna take that booty hostage.

"I hate you. You are the bad guy," she proclaimed. "You are the man that my mother warned me about, and I'll be damned if I let you ruin me."

"Damn it, Lawson, you passed the test!"

"Fuck you and yo' damn test!!" she exploded while loading her clothes into the suitcase. She was heated.

"Canieya," I said softly. "Canieya!"

"No. Not this time," she countered.

"We've been training vigorously for five years. Now I know I have done a lot of terrible things. Stupid things."

"Shut up, Crane," she interrupted, slamming the suitcase. "Your voice, your words are a deadly poison."

"Let me finish," I begged.

She whirled around briefly to see me standing in the doorway.

"I'm a criminal, the bad guy," I said. "I get it. It's just that I expect so much from you. You're just as great at being a law enforcer as I am at being a lawbreaker. That sounds crazy, but this glue has sat for too long. You can't just rip us apart because of one of my blundering choices. Why can't you see my true intentions here? How'd you expect this to end?"

She stared at me for a while as I stood there waiting for her to answer. Then she snatched up her oversized luggage and stormed toward me.

Standing firm, I tensed up to embrace her bulldozing demeanor. She stopped dead in my face.

"Tell me you don't love me," I cooed.

"Move," she mumbled as we stared at each other.

"Aren't you going to take me in?"

She didn't say a word. She just stood directly in my face,

breathing against my skin. Her hands shook with a hint of impatience as her eyes teared up. The zipper handles on her luggage trembled against one another. This light clanging sound reminded me of the occurrence.

Just then, an overwhelming gust of humbleness accessed my coiling sanity. My eyes closed to this traumatizing matter because I didn't use any empathy. And building up a resistance would only add insult to her injuries. As bad as I wanted her to stay, I had to discover what it meant to feel…

She stood in front of me, shaking and glaring into my eyes. Finally, I dropped my head and stepped aside.

She stood still, as my eyes fixed to the carpet.

"I want your *shit* out of my house," she grumbled, breathing fiercely.

Was a slap coming? With uncertainty, I tensed up in preparation. This suspenseful trail of waiting racked my conscience. What was running through her head? Was it over? Were we finished?

Her fierce blaze of breathing eased into a gentle, efficient flow of sweet air. Then I felt it again—a tensing like none other. I just knew that slap was coming. But instead, she firmly grabbed her luggage and stormed out of the bedroom.

She stomped towards the front door. Without hesitation, she yanked the door open and slammed it behind her.

Then the car cranked, and the car door shut.

Did I take too long to save the day? Maybe not…

That's when I rushed to the front door, and slung it open, and—

Wham!

She slapped the shit out of me.

Glittering stars and streaks of orange filled my vision. It took me a second to gather myself as she dropped her bags.

Stretching my jaw, I confessed, "I deserved th—"

—She jacked me up and kissed me roughly.

I lifted her up by her plump ass as she jumped in the air, wrapping her legs around me. She pressed the auto-crank button, turning off her car as I spun around.

Holding her tight, I slammed the front door closed.

She stopped kissing me, and she stared into my eyes. I looked back at her, and we connected like a plug in a socket.

We kissed vigorously as she tossed her keys into the adjacent hall.

She ripped me out of my shirt as I kissed on her neck. She melted away in affection. I carried her into the kitchen and sat her on the counter. She unbuckled my pants, discovering I was hard as a steel beam.

I grabbed a handful of her breast, and she clinched me in with her legs, digging deep into my boxers. She fondled me to her liking.

Ripping a hole in her black leggings, I dived, face first, into her puddle of moisture.

She moaned aloud as she toyed with my ears. Then I lifted her clean into the air while dancing my tongue about her sweet candy.

She yelled as she wrapped her legs around my shoulders. She squeezed my head tight with her thighs, then she scratched into my back.

"AAhhh… Fuck!" she hollered as her posture weakened. Her long, beautiful hair concealed her multiple expressions of glee.

I walked over to the coffee bar while still holding her up in the air. With her hips and her thighs resting above my shoulders, I gripped her tightly by her ass, then I sat her on the bar.

Gasping for air, Canieya released the grip in her thighs.

"Shit… I'm 'bout to cum."

I immediately stopped the warm, affectionate savoring of her all-you-can-eat buffet. She gripped me by my ears again, lifting my head up to her face. We kissed again, but this time it was full of juicy spit. She reached down to me again, rubbing my steel rod against her gooey center.

She laid her head in the refuge of my shoulders as she caressed herself. Then she licked in my ear and whispered seductively, "…Fuck me."

I laid my log deep into her campfire. The deeper I traveled, the tighter she gripped me with her legs. She got hot and extremely passionate. Grabbing her hair, I yanked her head back, and stroked away with consistency.

"Wait…," she said as she put her soft hands against my brick-hard chest. "I want to put on my heels."

But I couldn't say anything. Maybe because I kind of fancied the idea. My two-by-four flopped sloppily out of her runny tunnel as I backed away.

She stepped down from the coffee bar and hurried off to her room, taking off her shoes and leggings in the process.

Anxiously throbbing, staring down at myself, I propped up against the coffee bar. Then I heard a couple of drawers open and close. Right then her heels came a clocking. She appeared in the kitchen's entryway to see me bulging.

Canieya is half Japanese and half Black. Her golden skin tone and her thick brunette hair flowed well with her athletic build. Her smashing C-cup breast and those hazel eyes only complemented her hourglass figure. She had soft, high cheek bones with a small nose. Her elegant chin curved neatly into her jawline. And her full-figured lips could suck a man dry.

And now, Canieya was topless. She wore only a red silk garter belt and a pair of ultra-sheer, fully fashioned, skin tone stockings. She also had on a pair of red, open-toe mules with six-inch stiletto heels.

The exposing of her perfectly shaped body and circular, plump breasts only made things worse. For the appearance compounded my devilish thoughts.

She advanced forward with a giggle. She kneeled. Then she stared up into my eyes and snatched my shorts to my ankles, backing me into the coffee bar. She wrapped her mouth around my line of hope, leeching onto my metal railing.

She stood to her feet. Kissing me quickly, she mumbled, "Crane...I wanna have yo' baby."

Canieya shoved me back as I laid on the bar. Then she climbed on the countertop and stood over me with her hands on her hips. She looked down at me as her legs shivered.

She smelled so good, and her skin was so soft.

While standing to full attention, she turned around and

squatted on me without hesitation. Her aim was perfect as I slid in with finesse.

She hollered as she gripped her boobs, lifting her head to the ceiling. "Fuck!" she screamed while consuming me, inch by inch.

My arms wrapped around her waist. She closed her eyes and bit into her bottom lip.

"Fucking third arm, Crane," she said as I guided her up and down my plumbing shaft. "I love you…," she then admitted with teary eyes.

We kissed into each other as I penetrated her clouds of arousal.

Yeah, I fucked her—hid the salami with her, had sex with her, knocked boots with her, whatever you wanna call it with her— for at least four hours that day. It was the best makeup session a man of my stature could ever have.

A week later, in the misty dew of the morning, we laid next to each other in bed. She didn't look at me, and I didn't look at her. But we both knew what was happening. She sat up from under the sheets.

"I'm turning you in, Crane," she uttered. "Can't avoid this anymore… You are wanted in several states, and I am putting my future in danger by allowing you to go unpunished."

Finally, I rolled over to look in her face.

She smiled with a joking expression, but I didn't say anything.

"Just because I forgave you doesn't mean you get to treat me like that ever again," she inserted. "Next time, I will kill you and then turn you in. Plus, your farts smell like hair relaxer."

"Let's get married," I remarked.

She turned away from me. "That's out of the question. I'm taking this job in London."

"What if I quit? What if I stopped everything?" I pondered aloud.

She threw the sheets over my face as she climbed out of bed. "You're not about to change, Crane. And I'm running late for work."

"Can I get you some breakfast?" I yelled from under the sheets.

"What da' fuck! Did you not just hear me? I'm late already. No!" she complained as she rushed off to get her clothes.

Snatching the covers from over my head, I watched as she hurried off to the bathroom, closing the door behind her. Then I caught a glimpse of an object falling from her pants pocket.

Suddenly, she burst out of the bathroom and rushed over

to snatch up the item. Then she dashed back into the bathroom.

"Hey! What that wuz?" I quizzed as she slammed the door.

"Go da' hell!" she screamed.

AAhhh…yep! She loves me.

My thoughts settled as I rolled over to my back and linked my fingers behind my head. In return, I had fallen for her all over again. And even though we're exact opposites, with our night-and-day contradictory natures, we had found a way to coexist…

Twenty minutes later, Canieya came out of the bathroom with her head down. She tossed the object onto the bed and mumbled, "Congratulations, Crane"—she paused— "you're a father."

As I glanced down to the pregnancy test, she carried on as if it was nothing.

We didn't speak anymore that day.

Because of this odd unity, we had to raise Arla (Bookie) secretly. Man, I had to change my identity. We were just so restricted in our united fashion. Canieya covered up so much of our private lives that she became an asset. Our love had become too dangerous to persist. And I recall her saying it so plain and clear…

"Crane, I'm moving to London."

The idea was in our best interest. Mainly because her new assignment could put Bookie in the crosshairs. But in contrast, I wanted out of my criminal life and raising Bookie was the perfect excuse.

By the end of that third year, Canieya moved away. Honestly, the day she left was the day I became a full-time father. And for two years, without Canieya, I put my all into proper parenting.

* * *

CHAPTER: 5

Upturn
Part 1

| SaMeits Orbit xna | (transl) August 5, 2025- Present Day
Layo Galaxy, Upper Riaxon: Grand Valla

"Space Void will end soon," Simma said. "I'll wait here," he glanced over to Thorice. "patiently…"

Thorice nodded in agreement as Bail and Meth rushed over to the Teledeck. They stood on the teleportation device, and Bail nervously typed their destination into the control panel.

"Meth, my dear…," said Fice with a scraggly, degraded voice. "Tell my brother I await."

"Of course," Meth replied as the platform glowed.

Bail and Meth vanished.

Simma folded his arms and stared into the ceiling. Then he peeked over to see Thorice who could only stare in fear.

Thorice gulped.

Simma chuckled and stared back into the ceiling.

Thorice sprinted clean out of the building.

A thousand floors up Grand Valla, Bail and Meth materialized on the Teledeck.

They peered down the hall at the meeting room door. Then, stepping from the platform, they walked briskly through the hallway.

"My access code has changed. Do you have one," asked Meth.

"Yes, ma'am, I do," Bail replied.

A small stream of blood seeped from under the door as they approached.

"Open it." Meth ordered.

Bail entered the code and the door opened with ease.

The sacred room was lit by dozens of globes floating against the walls. They beamed in every shade of the sun. The floors and the partitions were made of platinum engravings. And at the head of this room sat a mighty window. Just in front of this window was the massive cybernetic table. The table came with various lights carved into the molecular makeup and into the matching chairs. But as the many lights brightened the room's opulence, so did they brighten this… grisly occasion.

"Ugk!" Bail vomited, engulfed by the ghastly smell. "Great inferno!"

Meth held out her hand. *ZzpK!!* - Lightning flashed out of her palm as a sphere oozed from her skin. While the poly sphere floated about, she shouted, "Go! Alert the others."

Bail dashed away as Meth glared back onto the massacre, "Fuck."

Meanwhile, Simma stood in the same position with his arms folded, and his eyes stapled to the ceiling- patiently awaiting his brother's return.

As the edges of the Teledeck illuminated, he opened his arms to embrace his brother. But instead, Bail materialized, tumbling off the Teledeck.

"Sir!" he screamed.

Simma looked down as Bail struggled awkwardly over the floor.

"What is it, lad? Doth my brother require my presence?" Simma quizzed as Bail looked up to him with watery eyes.

"No, sir…I—I don't know how else to say this, sir…" mumbled Bail.

"Aggh…spit it out, lad. On with it now!" Simma ordered.

"Your brother is dead, sir. He's dead!" shouted Bail.

"Ha!" Simma laughed.

"They're all dead, sir. Pias, Kuzar, Straton Mage. Dead, sir!" Bail hollered as he scrambled to his knees.

The feeling Simma once possessed shifted with profound disparity.

Thorice stuck his head in from the outside as several more officials entered the lobby.

Bail gagged again from the visually damaging experience.

"What the hell…?" Thorice asked as he walked back into the lobby.

Simma stood over Bail and said, "Take me, lad. Show me."

In the meeting hall, Meth whispered as she examined the horrors of Space Void. "An Auto Performing Admin…"

Meth reached into her compartment belt and took out a tiny flask. She walked over to the Feuler's seat and wiped up a slimy substance. Then she raked the substance into the flask and tucked it away. She peered under the large cybernetic table just when Thorice and Bail entered.

"Witness such violence…," Bail mumbled as he gestured into the room.

"Whaaahh the fuck," uttered Thorice.

Panic spawned into its true relevance as Meth walked slowly along the side of the table. While glancing up at the ceiling, she held out her hand, and the poly sphere sunk back into her palm.

She wiggled her toes in the bloody fluids.

"Something was here, close by," Meth grumbled as she wandered over to a delegate's corpse.

Simma had just approached the entry door when the officials stepped aside. As he entered, he immediately identified his brother.

"Velleyan," Simma uttered as he approached his brother's body.

Simma held up his hand, lifting his brother from the floor. The corpse floated over as he spread his fingers apart. Then the laceration in his brother's chest opened. As Simma gazed into the cavity, Meth lifted an Info Gram from the bloody floor.

Simma stared at his brother's body, wondering how this could've happened. Tuning everyone out, he bawled with an outpouring of tears, which fell vividly from his bloody eyes.

Meth approached his side and whispered. "Just finished decrypting this Info Gram. Does Lower Riaxon mean anything to you?"

"No," Simma replied as he continued to gaze at his brother's corpse.

"That was the last transmission received from this Info Gram's space proxy. And if I'm correct, the credits accrued from the same location," Meth deduced.

"Lower Riaxon," Thorice chattered.

"Notify your authorities," Meth ordered.

The officials moved with haste, but Bail, for some curious reason, stayed behind.

"Info Gram?" Bail asked.

"A particle-related device shrinkable in size for quick repository. Capable of infinite storage. Basically, a small-scale TPD," she answered. "I thought they were prohibited… like that Verne Gat," she pointed. "That weapon breaks all kinda Symbassy laws."

Bail scratched his forehead and smirked. "I'm in over my head, aren't I?"

"Yes. You are," Meth echoed as she peeped over her shoulder. "I dismiss you from further involvement. Please join the others."

Bail said nothing more as his presence became irrelevant. He dropped his head and hurried off to the Teledeck.

"Simma, I have something to show you," Meth said.

Fice dropped his hand, and his brother's body lowered to the floor.

Meth walked over to Simma. She reached into her compartment belt and took out the flask.

"This secretion is of slug descent," Meth said. "Judging by the texture, whoever did this had to be extremely old."

Simma sniffed and sobbed while gawking at his brother's body. And even though his face was covered, an obvious anger streamed from his eyes. Simma's vexation reeked above the stifling odor. "I've seen these paper-thin cuts before. A chef… at the Zygote, carries blades of antimatter, so thin that they vanish into nothing. So keen that they cut before contact."

"I don't get it…" Meth wondered. "Grand Valla, is one of the most luxurious structures in Riaxon. We are over a thousand stories into the Layian environment. This structure is made of pure diamond and topaz minerals. Every level has a Teledeck. The floors and the walls are thick as the Layain ground, which is a million times denser than diamonds and rubies. Checkpoints surrounded this guarded structure. Each room is airtight, enlarged, and soundproofed for secrecy. How could something like this even occur?"

Simma scowled…

"My father's death powers my passion for revenge. Nothing will stop me from rendering Arola justice," Meth said. "But this… This wasn't Arola. This was something else. A major modification to the Symbassy's timetable. This inaugurates war. It will affect every society on every planet that we've colonized," Meth proclaimed as she put the flask back into her utility pocket. "Mr. Fice, I can notify the Xaris and dispatch a team to Lower Riaxon within a half sun cycle."

"Make it so," Simma cried as he kneeled over his brother's body. His eyes filled with bloody tears. "My brother, I will avenge you, and I will bury this fiend next to you." Then, he reached to his wrist and typed into a sleek diamond gauntlet. A transparent monitor opened over his forearm.

"Elitex. Expedite Rapture." Simma ordered as the small monitor flashed.

> *"Opening TPD gateways for planet mobilization. Would you like to activate Hit List-protocol?"*

"Yes," Simma confirmed as he stood.

"Hit List-Activated."

He then lowered his forearm and the small monitor closed.

"You *do* know what this means, don't you?" Meth asked with sincerity.

Simma peeped over his shoulder and replied with a voice of fury. "… Yes. Genocide…"

CHAPTER: 6

Student of the Month

August 5, 2025- Present Day
The Bronx, New York: Pine Wood Magnet School

"And the student of the month award goes to..." Principal Millard shouted as she opened the envelope. "...Arla Lawson!"

Oh my God! I lit up. I jumped out of my seat, high-fiving other parents as they sat befuddled. I was so glad because I felt as though I was succeeding as a parent.

The pianist played while Bookie skipped across the stage.

"Yeah!" I shouted as she curtseyed to the crowd.

"This award has been given to you for showing signs of a dedicated, smart, and inspiring student," announced Principal Millard. "In addition, you show gifts and elements of leadership with a humbleness that will forever encourage the staff and body of Pine Wood Magnet School."

"Damn right!" I shouted from the rear of the school's newly remodeled gymnasium.

Bookie smiled so hard when she received her award.

I used the crowd's applause as my opportune moment to jet down the aisle. I stood in front of the stage, taking pictures with my smartphone.

As Bookie exited the stage, the pianist stopped playing.

Soon, an awkward silence tamped down the crowd's enthusiasm. Mainly because I was still taking pictures like a photographer during a photoshoot.

"That's my girl!" I yelled with several claps mixed in among the echoes.

Bookie was only five, and she had been accelerating in her academics for a while. I wouldn't have it any other way. She was going to be great. I saw her changing the world.

Afterward, Bookie and I sat outside, chillin' on the steps of the now vacant school.

"Oh! I almost forgot." Bookie smiled as she dug into her backpack. She took out a piece of folded paper and handed it to me.

"What's this?" I quizzed as I unfolded the paper.

"That's me on the left. You in the middle. And…" She paused as I turned the page over.

"Why is there an *X* over mommy?"

"Well, I think you need another girlfriend," she answered. "Daddy, I did good in school?"

"Yep," I responded as I tucked the image into my coat pocket. "Couldn't be any prouder."

"Are you going to send pictures to Mommy?"

"Oh yeah! I can do that," I said reluctantly as I took out my phone, hoping that she would change the subject.

Just then, my phone rang. Ah! Saved by the bell. "Hello? Quincy. Yeah, what's up? Sure thing. Give me 'bout forty-five minutes."

St. Patrick's Cathedral
New York, NY

The gorgeous interior of the cathedral was filled with elaborate walls and paintings. The floors were spotless, and the pews were overall uncomfortable. But the lighting throughout the cathedral was dim and very calming on the eyes.

"We're all the same, Derrick," Quincy whispered from the confines of his rustic confession booth. "The only thing that changes with extreme certainty is the organism—through the process of evolution. The fact that an organism may start out in one form and develop into another, is an undeniable transformation. We are all living proof of such a supposition. Do you think Darwin would have ignored the signs if they had been put right in his face? No! Of course not."

Now, Quincy Harmon—or Father Harmon—and I go way back. 'Bout a couple of years ago, I was passing by, and I saw a bunch of ladies rushing in the church. I followed them in, thinking it was some kind of gothic nightclub or something. After stepping foot into the cathedral, I noticed Father Harmon standing on the other side of the doors. He was like, "Chasing that ass, huh?"

We've been hanging ever since.

He's always had a gust of energy, a spryness about him

that would make the average middle-aged man jealous. He had taken care of himself throughout his years as a human. He's one of those older guys with a six-pack. I wouldn't know. He told me one time that he had just turned fifty-seven, but I think he meant seventy-five.

He stood a few inches taller than me. His skin was wrinkle-free. He had a big nose, an odd-shaped head, and sharp, piercing eyes that compel you to tell the truth. He had all of his teeth. And what was really odd was that Father Harmon had all of his hair. And without a single gray strand. Still, after meeting with Quincy on several occasions, I found the old geezer to be a friend.

You see, as a kid I was bullied. Mom dukes caught dad cheating. Shot him in the head then killed herself. And I saw the whole thing. Ever since then, I've had suicidal thoughts. To free my head, I joined several gyms and took a few self-defense classes. That wasn't enough. The streets took me. Got addicted to crack. Joined a gang. Got involved with the Mob. The list goes on. Honestly, I hoped that someone would off me. Because I just couldn't do it myself. When I met Canieya, my life flipped. Then Bookie came. That's when I developed another meaning and Father Harmon had a way of quenching my suicidal spirit.

Anyways, I don't get into all that…you know, religion stuff. I'm just not that big on it. But Quincy is. He's big on outer space, aliens, and the afterlife, too. I think Scientology would be more fitting.

"Society continues to emerge, so does the chemical makeup of the human brain. Yet areas of the human brain are not readily accessible to man. They have been locked away because most humans wouldn't wield the powers of the brain appropriately," he explained as I sat in the dark confession booth next to him.

"Derrick, I have met with you several times now, and all I am getting is a lot of anger, sadness, and hatred. I want to help you, Derrick, but I can't rewrite your past. However, I can assist you in finding peace with your future." The wise clergyman man then changed the subject. "How's Bookie?"

"Ah, she's fine. Sitting in one of them ungrateful-ass pews."

"That's bad. But back to this brain power stuff. There's a guy that plays for the Giants. He stays upstate. He and I are pretty good friends."

"Okay…?"

"This guy is said to be, and I believe he is, the fastest thing on Earth," Quincy boasted. "I believe this man has special access to his brain. And I want you to meet him."

I didn't know what to say.

"How fast is the fastest man? Don't answer that," he continued. "C'mon, Derrick. Don't you like football?"

"UUUUgghhhh… man. I don't know."

"Don't answer that either, then. I tell you what… How about I take you to meet him?" he insisted. "You'll be impressed with this phenomenon. And if you're not, then maybe the social interaction will free you from some of these suicidal thoughts. Start the process of inner peace."

"All right…," I muttered. "But I'm bringing Bookie."

"Ha! I knew you'd say that!" the clergyman shouted. "Time's up." He then stepped out of the booth, slamming the confession window shut at the same time.

Father Harmon and his wisdom showered over me as I sat in confusion. Obviously, this was a dumbass deal.

Then he cracked open my confession booth door. A soft light riddled through the dusty fragments floating into the booth. "You coming out?" he barked.

The clergyman stood in front of me holding the door open with a huge smile on his face. "Let's meet here around six in the morning," he said as I finally got up.

"Man, that's too early," I claimed with my usual negative attitude. "Bookie still go be sleep."

"Daddddddyyyy!!!" Bookie shouted from a distance. "This pew making my ass hurt!"

"My word." The clergy glared with a mumble, "Who she get that from?"

"Aw man. Look at the time!" I chuckled as I hurried out of the confession booth.

Quincy turned to me and smiled, while holding that Bible of his. "What else you got to do?" he asked. "Hey, I'll buy breakfast."

"Deal. Bookie!!" I shouted while beckoning for her.

She leaped from the pew and sprinted up to my side, giggling. "Let's go, Daddy."

"Hey man!" Quincy shouted in joyous laughter. "I love you, and so does God! And there's nothing you can do about it! Don't you stand me up, Derrick!" He waved as we exited.

CHAPTER: 7

The Dunlos

August 6, 2025
New York, NY

Before the crack of dawn, an all-black '79 Impala sat on the curb of the cathedral. The sleek vehicle revved over a set of Daytons, while a thin smoke gurgled from its snarling pipes.

When I arrived, it was six a.m. on the dot. After grabbing Bookie from the back seat, I walked over to Father Harmon's car. I opened the rear passenger door and sat Bookie into the cozy leather seat.

"She *is* still asleep," Quincy noted as I buckled her in and shut the door.

After opening the passenger door, I sat briefly into the seat. Now, I expected Father Harmon to be in civilian clothing. But he was still in that same black robe, with that same white collar-thing. He dropped a small paper bag into my lap and pointed to the cup holder next to me.

"That's your hot chocolate," he advised as a light steam rose from the lid.

I opened the small bag to see two glazed doughnuts. "This your idea of breakfast?" I retorted with critical taste.

"These are the best doughnuts in America. You know I was a stunt driver in my past life," he included as he shifted the gear and floored the gas pedal.

Granite Springs, New York

A while later, we approached the speed demon's mansion.

The gates to the domain were incredibly massive. A large lion head was emblazoned on the center of the oversized gate.

We stopped momentarily at the call box. "Quincy!" shouted a voice from the box.

"Hey, brother! We're here," Quincy answered.

The large gates opened slowly, and we entered the stunning, magnificent spread. The exuberant and carefully maintained lawn zapped my troubled mind. The escape was priceless. His yard was full of exotic plants coupled with hundreds of different flowers.

"They got a doctor or a scientist or something out here to evaluate his speed," Quincy explained. "Name starts with a *P*. Pansler? Or Paxton? I don't know."

It took us nearly five minutes just to approach the front porch of the mansion. Glaring upon the edifice, my eyes wandered up to the view and my jaw dropped to the floor. The entire house was made of marble, and a host of massive pillars supported the frontal structure. The sight pulled a genuine response out of me.

"WWwwhhhhhoooaaaa…" I ogled in amazement.

"Oh yeah. They laid, man," Quincy chuckled as he parked. "I'm telling you, Derrick, this guy ain't normal. I think he gets faster as he runs, like a machine or something."

I really didn't care to see the speedster's talent. But I was overly impressed with the house, though. Just then, a soft stir came from the backseat.

"Daddy, is that a Tacca Chantrieri?" whispered Bookie with a yawn.

"Yes, it is. Yes, it is…," I answered. Really, I didn't know what the fuck she was talking 'bout.

We piled out of the car and approached the oversize double doors.

"Whoa! That's a big door," Bookie said.

"Sometimes I don't know if he's coming or going." Quincy said. "I'm telling you now, this cat ain't normal."

"They have a cat?" Bookie quizzed.

"Just promise me you'll be nice. Please?" Quincy pleaded as he looked over to me.

Then I looked down to Bookie and grabbed her hand. But before I could respond, the door swung open.

"AAAahhhh! Quincy! My main man," hollered Corey.

"Yes, sir!" Quincy replied.

They embraced each other with a strong manly hug, slapping each other on the back. Then they stepped away in laughter.

"And who is this?" Corey asked.

"Oh, forgive me," Quincy said. "This is Derrick Lawson. You know, the guy I've been telling you about."

"No… not him." The speedster pointed at Bookie. "You! Who the hell is you?"

"Arla Lawson, sir!" Bookie answered as she held out her hand. "Pleasure to meet you."

"Uh huh…" Corey shook her little hand while I focused on his face.

He was tall as Quincy and his hair was low and full of waves. He was younger—a lot younger—and his skin was much darker. His nose was thin, and his eyes were very odd. They seemed glitchy, as if they were flashing. But he was very athletic. It was more than obvious that he was all about football.

Just then, the Earth stood still…

The planet and the sun lost their logic of gravitation.

I felt the ground moving and shaking around me. Yet, there was no earthquake.

My heart and eyes stopped, and I couldn't turn my head or blink my eyes. This sight was so spellbinding.

I heard angels singing along with a host of bells, performing a song with radical lyrics. It carried over the speed demon and Father Harmon's conversation. The joyous sound was so loud that I couldn't tell if they were still talking.

As I peered deep into the speedster's mansion, my stomach churned, and my heart splashed into my belly. Then the image clarified. I saw an elegant swan. A woman. A beyond angelic masterpiece with a gorgeous grade of natural dark brown hair. A crafty, curly afro, surrounded in clean moisture. Her skin and complexion were without stain or blemish. It was like the color of a bright sun tapping the noon sky.

As the lioness approached, I was able to digest the pleasure of her aesthetics.

Her nose was small, and her jawline and chin curved with a silky-smooth wave of sexy. Her ears and cheekbones complimented her eyes, which were light gray with a hint of blue.

Her colors were so natural, vivid, and beguiling. I could not escape such beauty. She was mixed with another race that I couldn't identify. Yet race had no concern to her moment of majesty.

She had a walk that could nullify a trillion dollars.

Priceless.

She wore a fitted, black sleeveless dress that stopped mid-thigh, almost right above her knees. The top of her dress had a small V-cut in the chest area, revealing a bit of her cleavage.

She was probably five-five or five-six with a small waist.

Her curves were all strategically placed.

She was very athletic, too. Her legs and calf muscles were clearly defined. She had on a pair of sheer black nylons and some six-inch black stilettos. The front of her shoes came to a point. That meant she was classy and somewhat business savvy, by my interpretation.

"Oh my, she's pretty," Bookie whispered as the goddess reached the doorway.

My thoughts and desires left me in a labyrinth. Because I knew I was lusting for the speedster's wife. She was a must-have. And she was ten times better than Canieya, and I considered Canieya to be a ten.

But this woman, this queen, had no grading scale.

The speedster kissed the goddess on her forehead as she cautiously passed.

"Take it easy, Sis," the speedster encouraged with a gleam in his eye.

Who kisses their wife on the forehead?

Wait a minute…

Did he just say... Sis?

Holy shit!

It's on.

I froze, stiffer than an inanimate object as the goddess passed between us.

"Excuse me," she softly chimed as she glanced up to me.

Her voice was so deliquescing and sweet. Her airy larynx could turn rocks into *Play-Doh*. But her exit had not fully completed.

I was hit again.

A smell so beatifically luring and tropically searing, it could make a steak sweat. Like the smell of a new car mixed with a luxurious female pheromone, so strong that she could affect a man's behavior in the next state. And I sucked it all in.

My body rocked, tantalized by the concluding mellow gust. I felt myself fainting…

"Good day, Okani," said Quincy.

"Good day, Father," the woman replied as she continued to her car.

"Bye, pretty lady!" Bookie waved as the goddess made her exit.

"Goodbye, little queen," Okani answered with a sweet gesture.

For a second, I looked forward, fighting my urge to turn

around… Aaaggghh, fuck it!

Her ass wasn't big or bodacious, but it was perfect and a tad bit larger for a woman of her size. She was simply incredible.

"Aw shit, fellas," hollered the speed demon. "Where are my manners? Come the fuck in. Come in!"

This dude cursed way more than me. I, however, was still watching Okani as she opened the door to her red sports car.

Quincy grabbed my shoulder. He turned me around to see the speedster, gesturing for us to enter.

"What y'all want to eat? I got some deer meat shit in the fridge. I'll get Lurch to whip y'all up some damn deer sausage. Y'all want some deer sausage?" Chatted the speedster.

"That sounds disgusting," Bookie answered as we entered.

"Didn't nobody ask you," the speedster blurted. "You wanna see how fast I am?"

Bookie answered with a frown. "Let's see what you got!"

Sometime later and several floors below, in the speedster's basement, I sat baffled in a black plush leather recliner.

This basement of his was a fully functioning gym. There were free weights, elliptical machines, punching bags, full-body mirrors, squat racks, huge medicine balls, bar benches, treadmills, and twenty-inch flat screens.

I was outdone. Not by this awesome gym, but by this…

Okani.

While Bookie frolicked about the kids' room next door, I viewed with no true interest as the speedster jogged away on a treadmill. Father Quincy and a doctor from Queens accompanied him. They, in contrast, watched earnestly during this unexplainable event. They believed that the speedster's strand of muscular madness could, perchance, unleash a momentum of no end.

"Corey, as strange as this may sound, has a segmented meter range between zero to twenty off the blocks," the scientist explained. "Most runners' speeds decrease over the course of a set race. Now, the drag also comes at the start of the race. The reaction time, wind, plus the moment in achieving actual acceleration can all contribute to a runner's lag. I think if Corey was to have a continuous surge of energy, he could probably run up to—and even over one hundred meters—in about six-point-five to seven seconds flat."

"Now, Doc, what's your name again?" Quincy asked.

"Phlaxlur."

"Oh yeah. That's crazy, right?" queried Father Quincy. "How can a human run that fast?"

"According to the theory of evolution, it is quite plausible, especially if the DNA of a human has been properly fed and nourished throughout a particular family's lineage. Anything then becomes biologically suitable," Phlaxlur acknowledged while holding his clipboard. He monitored the equipment as they received readings from a host of adhesive pads attached to Corey's arms, chest, and head.

"Damn right! I'll catch a cheetah," roared the speedster as I sat with my mouth wide open, staring into the ceiling. "Fact is, I've blown every recruiter's mind. Wacky ain't it? Don't wait, homie! Weight broke down the wagon. I'm 'bout to throw your mind in the air and catch it!"

"My dad can do that!" Bookie shouted from a far.

Frankly, I was so separated from the world that I began to question myself.

Every time I closed my eyes, I saw her floating in an amorphous sea of red pumps and silk sheets. What a gorgeous presence. Okani had my heart thumping. I was being strangled by amour. Cupid had me in a chokehold.

Canieya and I were just a fling, an infatuation that extended way beyond what I originally expected. I thought for sure that I may have been in love with Canieya. But I'd never felt like this. Why was this happening?

As thousands of love songs swirled through my brain, I found it hard to place a specific song with my Okani. She was too genuine.

Man! I didn't want to think that I was in love, but…

"Fuck!" I spontaneously blurted.

"Egh, hey, hey!" shouted the speedster.

The doctor and Father Harmon were both looking at me like I was crazy.

Corey jogged away, pointing over to the wall adjacent to me. "You see that jug over there?" he asked.

I glanced at him and then back to Quincy.

"Nnnoooo… over there, man!" shouted Corey as he pointed even harder.

Then, over to the wall to my right, I saw a big flat-screen television.

"Look down. On top of the entertainment center," the speed demon instructed.

And there, where he'd been pointing, rested a large five-gallon plastic jug. On the front of this jug was a piece of gray tape with SWEAR JUG written on it. The jug was full of cash and coins.

With anger I turned to face Corey.

He was still pointing at the plastic jug when he spoke with a grimacing tone. "You go have to put some money in that fucking jug, homie."

Ohhh… I blew up!

"Man, mutha' fuck yo' jug!" I screamed as I rushed over to the container.

Phlaxlur hugged his clipboard as Father Quincy started shaking his head, giving me a cut-it-out gesture with his hand.

I snatched up the bucket with one hand and launched it into the TV.

THdnK!!

The jug cracked the screen, snaking a rift through the glass. With violent whomps, the jug bounced about the room, slinging money everywhere.

"Derrick!" Quincy yelled as I picked the jug up again and banged it across the speedster's equipment.

Father Harmon started to come over, but he stopped in his tracks.

Turning back around, I threw the jug across the way. And

that's when Bookie came out of the kids' room. The jug bounced and rolled over the floor. It settled next to her foot as she stood beside the squat rack.

My nose flared as I stood there, huffing.

Father Quincy dropped his head, and the doctor kept looking at me as he backed into the corner.

Just then, Corey stopped running and the treadmill tossed him clean off the conveyor belt.

This happened so fast that the wires plucked from the adhesive patches.

The speedster landed with accuracy onto the black-matted floor. He stood upright and looked over to me, right when Bookie approached his side and said, "My daddy can do that too."

"Shit, man. I'm 'bout to be late for practice," Corey blurted, drying his face with a nearby towel. "Wrap it up, Doc."

Dr. Phlaxlur picked up the severed wires and looked at them for a short moment. Then he gracefully dropped the cords and began to shut off his devices.

The speedster walked over to Quincy quickly.

"I'm sorry, Corey. I didn't see this coming," Quincy noted in sorrow.

"Look, Q, I'm sorry about having to roll out so fast, but I wasn't aware of the time. Shit be shifting, ya dig?" the speedster snarled as he glared at me, rolling his eyes back over to Father

Harmon as he reached into his jogging pants. "I gotta take a shower. Hey? Do me a favor, right?"

"Anything, Corey." Quincy replied.

The speed demon pointed at me, flopping out his penis. "You!" he yelled.

Quincy covered Bookie's eyes, shouting, "Mary and Jesus."

"Suck. My! Dick!" Corey yelled.

I rushed him in anger. As the speedster tucked his penis away, Dr. Phlaxlur darted in, holding me back.

Then the speedster pulled out a wad of money with several rubber bands wrapped around it. He yanked off the bands, that plucked away with tiny snaps.

"Put this in the swear jug," he ordered, handing Quincy the hunk of money.

The clergyman slowly lifted his hand from Bookie's eyes. And with guarded motions, Quincy took the cash and walked over to the swear jug.

Dr. Phlaxlur trekked back over to his equipment as I finally settled.

"That's for me and you," Corey muttered as he pointed at me and himself. He then dashed up the stairs.

"Can I open my eyes now?" Bookie asked.

"Yes," Quincy answered.

"Oh!" shouted the speedster as he spun around, jumping from the top of the stairs. He landed a few inches shy of his original spot while Bookie and I scraped up the cash.

Father Harmon came over with the swear jug tucked under his arm, mumbling "Both of yawl… *stealing?*"

He glared on as we stuffed the cash into our pockets.

"I know this little display didn't provide any real answers," the speedster said as he turned to face Father Harmon. "How about I give you two some VIP passes to the game. Consider it done. All right?" Then he flew up the stairs.

As the broken television glitched in the background, Father Quincy looked at me and dropped his head in disappointment.

Phlaxlur was still in the background unplugging his machines at a sad, but quick pace. I knew he was pissed because the athlete snatched out all the wiring with his erratic dismount. I wondered if Corey knew he still had a few pads sticking to him.

That's when Bookie walked over to me with a hand full of twenties. She leaned in and whispered, "How much you got?"

Moments later, near the front door to the speed demon's mansion, Father Quincy, Bookie, and I stood in the foyer. The clergyman felt... well, I guess he found it necessary to somewhat scold me for my deranged outpouring.

I hope Quincy would choose his words wisely because I was unstable and the only one here with mental issues. The speedster, however, may have been a bit worse than me. He was real jacked up and I don't think anyone cared.

But above all, I felt reserved. I felt sort of jolly. Bookie was humbling me. And all I could see now was…

Okani.

And even though the goddess had been gone for over an hour now, I could still smell her, plain as day.

"Hey!" someone yelled from a distance.

Quincy and I turned around, looking in unison to the top of the stairs.

There stood Corey… completely naked.

We snatched away from the sighting as I covered Bookie eyes. "Again?" she whined.

"Y'all 'bout to leave?" Corey yelled.

"Man, go put yo' clothes on. Shit!" I hollered.

"I'm just saying, though —" The speedster continued to jabber in riddles as Father Harmon spoke over him.

"Corey has a phobia," he said. "He's afraid of time and clocks."

"That don't mean he get to pop up naked!" I retorted as I glanced over to the living room.

The speed demon was now fully dressed and sitting on top of a white leather couch playing video games. That's when I uncovered Bookie's eyes.

"I got five minutes to kill your ass. You a supa' bitch!" he hollered while tapping on the remote control.

"What is he talking about?" Bookie asked.

"This my land hoe! Egh lil' girl!" yelled the speedster. "You wanna cut some grass?"

"No, thank you," Bookie replied

"I gotta plenty of grass to cut. Oh shit! Dis hoe dun tried to clip my ass. Take dat hoe! YEeeeahhhh!"

Father Harmon was right. Corey had a noticeably short attention span. He was unhinged and all over the place.

"He's going to shock the world, Derrick. Tell me you're going to the game…" Quincy spoke.

"Yeah…I'll go. I ain't got nothing better to do," I said.

I thought I would see Okani again. Then, suddenly, a butler walked over to greet us. He was holding a solid gold tray with two black envelopes on it. Our names had been engraved on each envelope.

"Compliments of Corey Dunlo," the butler announced.

"Take that shit, Q!" shouted the speedster from the living room. "You better be there, too, crazy guy!"

"Thanks, Corey. We'll be there. Right, Derrick?" the clergyman asked while turning to me.

"Yeah…," I mumbled.

"Can I come?" Bookie asked.

Thunk!

"Gotcha, bitch!" Corey hollered, having spiked the remote to the floor.

"Na. But you can hang with Tom." I answered.

"Aw man…," cried Bookie.

"What? I thought you like chilling with the neighbor." I said as Quincy took the envelopes from the golden tray. The butler bowed then walked away gracefully.

Father Harmon handed me my envelope, as the doctor approached. You could hear him coming with all those crates and durable cases.

"You guys mind getting the door for me?" he asked.

"Sure," Quincy offered and turned to open the doors. But the doors were already opening. Quincy came to a pause.

"Are these doors automated?" the clergyman asked as a soft breeze flowed out of the manor. He then turned to the doctor. "And what's your name again? I keep forgetting."

The doctor stopped to answer Father Harmon. "Phlaxlur. Dr. Phlaxlur. And no, the doors are not automated."

"That's what it is. I knew your name started with a *P*," Quincy said.

The doctor laughed as he secured his equipment. "Well… later, huh?"

That's when I noticed a subtle glitch in Phlaxlur's eyes as he hurried out of the mansion. It was that same odd glint I'd seen in the speedster's eyes.

"See ya, Corey. And thanks again," yelled Dr. Phlaxlur.

The clergyman motioned for me to exit as he held the door open. I took Bookie by the hand.

And just as we exited, Father Quincy jumped back. "Whoa!"

"Shit!" I hollered as Bookie jumped behind me.

Corey the speedster was standing outside, right beside the door. He was leaning against the marble wall with his arms folded, using his shoulder to support his weight.

The clergyman grabbed his chest as if he was going into

cardiac arrest.

"Question," said the speedster.

Bookie and I took a double-take, back into the living room. He had just been playing video games. But now, no one was there. The TV had been turned off and the video game system was neatly put away.

I gawked back at him with my eyes wide open.

"Why you wanna kill yourself?" he asked.

Bookie stared up to me as I dropped my head. The question asked too much. It was a revelation, correlating with his amazing speed.

It made me sprint, mentally, increasing my warping. My thoughts were traveling too fast for me to answer this... this question.

"It's a conundrum, ain't it? Almost as fast as me. Almost." He giggled.

He then stepped closer to Quincy and me, unfolding his arms, he mumbled, "Nothing is worse than a powerful man with no goals, no ambition, no purpose."

Then he snatched Bookie's drawing out of my coat pocket. He did it so fast, it felt like he punched me in the chest.

"What the hell is this?" Corey asked while unfolding the image. "You drew this?"

"No." Bookie giggled. "Daddy can't draw at all."

The speedster looked over the image briefly and grumbled, "Trash." Then he ripped the drawing to shreds.

"Hey!" Bookie shouted.

"That's for wrecking my gym. Get the fuck on. Less you wanna cut some grass. Jewell!" Corey hollered.

I started to get angry but Quincy kept patting my back.

Clenching the torn image in his fists, Corey pointed out to his lawn while peeping into the living room. "Jewell!! We gotta lotta grass to cut!" Then, he glanced over to me. "Can you believe her name is Jewell?"

I was finna deck Corey in the face, but he said something that threw me into next week. "My sister has a crush on you."

"I knew it!" Bookie hollered.

"You aint know shit," the speedster replied just as a maid rushed to his side.

"Yes sir?" said Jewell.

"Jewell!" he screamed. "Where you get that name from?"

"My parents, sir."

"Put this shit in the trash," he ordered, dumping the shredded image into her hands.

She kneeled to gather the portions that fell. Then she

stood up fast, bowing away with an elegant courtesy.

"Na, naa… put it in the swear jug," the speedster clarified.

"Yes sir," she answered as she rushed off.

"That's my picture…" Bookie whined.

"Y'all still here?" Corey asked. Then, he stepped over to my ear and whispered. "You know I can be in two places at once. Probably three." He then glared down as Bookie tugged on his pant leg.

"My dad can do that too." She grumbled. "He can beat you so bad, you'll be playing drums with Twizzlers for a week."

The speedster darted into his mansion without a word.

"I'm coming back for my picture!" Bookie shouted as the door slammed.

Ka-Floommmm!!

Quincy smirked, "Crazy guy, ain't he?"

"He tore up my picture!" Bookie said as we walked away.

"Cut that damn grass, Lurch." The speedster hollered from behind the door. "What the fuck!"

For five minutes, I looked at the speedster's lawn in passing to encounter a soothing peace. As we approached the huge gates, the clergyman begun to slow down. He was staring hard at something. We both stared with incredulity as a silhouette came into view near the lion-headed gate. There he was… the speedster.

"What the hell," I grumbled.

With his arms folded, he leaned against the column, as he'd done earlier. He shook his head as we passed through the massive gates.

CHAPTER: 8

Upturn
Part 2

Layo Galaxy, Upper Riaxon
Grand Valla's Landing Pad

Several suns brightened the small cockpit of Meth's clunky space craft as she paced the floor. She sat abruptly into the pilot seat, slumped over the control desk and grabbed her face. She peered through the ship's windshield.

"Fuck," she hollered, reaching for her TPD. She activated the device and a monitor displayed above the ship's control desk.

"Yesss…"

"What the **fuck**, Feuler?!" Meth shouted into the display. "I told you to convey and recon. **Convey** and **recon**!"

"It was his idea. No, it wasn't," the Feuler replied.

"Shit man, are you *trying* to blow my cover?"

"I don't blow- That's not what I heard. Shut it!" the Feuler rambled.

"Dude, I saved those schematics on a drive. All you had to do was hand it to 'em."

"Yeah."

"So…? Where the fuck is the drive?"

"He ate it."

"God damn it," Meth scolded as she hopped from the pilot seat, pacing roughly across the small bridge. "I wish I knew… Feuler," she snickered. "Im having a hard time accepting this shit." She stopped and propped herself up on the back of the pilot seat. "Convey and recon, Feuler. Not butcher a group Xarchanzians." Meth grabbed her face. "Ahw, shit man. SHiittt!!! Fuck!!" she hollered pacing over the bridge again. "You killed Pias, *and* Velleyan Fice?"

"They got in the way."

"Do you even know who Velleyan Fice is?"

"Uhhh…"

"That's Simma Fice's brother. Simma is one of the most feared Xarchanzians in the Layo Galaxy. And you just killed his only brother. He's coming for you. They're **all** coming for you. You *do* know that right?"

"I didn't… I did!"

"We are so fucked right now. I can't fix this."

"Are you done? …Probably not," the Feuler said.

"Fucking A. The Xaris are everywhere. They'll exterminate us, Feuler. Fuck man… you just started a **war**! Every thriving planet will feel it."

"You shouldn't have asked," the Feuler muttered.

Click!

He terminated the call.

Meth gawked into the fading display. She plopped back into the pilot seat and glared over to her Moly Board resting on the floor, and against the control desk.

This damnable weapon absorbs pressure and redistributes a heavier mass, resulting in a trail of rebounding destruction. The stellar racket is forged from Dark Matter and Tierun. Its black oval frame glowed with fiery solar flares, streaking through its crackly design and into the bulky handle. Assembled near the top of its formation was a creepy blue sphere, that swirled ever so lightly inside the dense racket's frame.

Meth glanced away in thought, staring back out of the ship's windshield. She grabbed her TPD again…

Layo Galaxy: Arola's Citadel
The Fact Matter Room

The atmosphere of this gloomy expanse blossomed with vibrant floating equations. A legion of scientist worked from their desks while an omnipotent being sat at the head of this massive room.

He lolled in a luxurious throne comprised of precious stones. In deep thought did he ponder when a monitor popped up beside his head.

The mad titan peeped over to the screen. He grabbed the transparent monitor with both hands and said, "Phlaxlur."

At that moment, a doctor stood in the rear of this massive room. He travelled through the ocean of scientist and up to the titans' throne. With his head lowered, the doctor uttered, "Yes, my liege."

While yet studying the holographic screen the titan ordered, "Initiate Project MOS."

Phlaxlur peeped to the floor and with a shady smile…

CHAPTER: 9

MI-6

August 7, 2025
Wimbledon, London, United Kingdom

My phone rang at 4:30 a.m.

Rolling over in my cozy bed, I picked up the phone and placed it to my ear.

"Lawson! Lawson! What in god's name are you doing?"

Damn, Chief Goodrum. He was nothing like the other guy, who died tragically in a drug sting a couple of years ago.

"Hello," I mumbled.

"I need you in early. I'll —"

"Goody, I don't come in for another three hours. What's the problem?"

"I'll explain it to you when you get here. Get up! Drink some black coffee!" he ordered, hanging up the phone.

Now it was too early for Goody's confusing riddles. It seemed like he was excited about something.

Finally, I hung up the phone and got out of the bed.

After jumping into the shower, I got dressed fast. Then I proceeded into the kitchen, to prepare some horrible coffee. Quickly, I poured the coffee into my silver canteen. Then I rushed out of the house.

Stepping into the cold of the day, I shut the house door and locked it behind me.

While jogging to the car, I pressed the auto start on my keychain. After taking a sip of coffee, I paused to open the car door and a light flickered through the window.

I spun with a gasp, dropping my canteen as a figure vanished from my rooftop. While peering at the roof, my canteen rolled down the driveway.

For a moment I focused on the area, but nothing was there. After grabbing my canteen from the ground, I plopped in the seat of my car. After slamming the car door, I examined the rooftop again. I put the car in reverse and eased out of the driveway while an eerie, spooky essence nestled in the sunless pits of my dawning day…

Vauxhall, London
MI-6 Headquarters

Man, you talking about chaos. Shit, it seemed like every human on the force had been called in. With such an upheaval, I didn't know what to expect, so I strode confidently as I approached the entrance doors.

With a deep breath, I walked into my paradise and the office turbulence slowed to a lurch…

"Oh, don't get quiet now! Acting like you saw a ghost or something," I boomed as I walked over to my desk.

Crashing into my seat, I sighed with relief. Then I reached in my purse for my pocket mirror. After checking my nose, I put the mirror away and kicked my feet up on the desk. I stared off into this space of junk, orange hazing, musty skank of an office. As my memories unscrambled and reformed in order, I thought about Crane. The memory alone triggered my crazy.

Whom!

A slamming door interrupted my thoughts.

My head lifted to notice my short and stocky, bald-headed boss standing in front of his office.

He walked over to my desk as I glanced down to my purse.

But when I looked up, he was standing right over me.

I smirked. "You know, if you really want to startle someone, try sending them a naked photo."

"Very funny." He chortled, then leaned into my ear and whispered, "My office. Now."

Goody's office had the same orange haze as the rest of the building. The only difference was the cigar smoke that soared triumphantly over the odor. My hesitant nature disappeared as he sat at his desk.

"I saw a ninja staring at me from my rooftop," I told him.

"There's no such thing as ninjas," he replied. "Especially not in London. Have a seat—but don't make yourself at home."

"What's that supposed to mean?" As I sat down, I took a piece of gum from my pocket.

"Horace Vaydin just blew up a police precinct in New York," said Goody.

"You can't be serious… How?"

"Quite simple. He got a copy of the blueprints and planted a series of C4 explosives around the base of the structure."

"No warning or ransom, ultimatum, or anything?"

"Nope. Next thing you know, every floor was reduced to rubble. This is the fifth time this year the US Federal Agency has called me, begging for some assistance. People are dropping dead left and right. This man got half of the nation looking for him.

Bounty hunters, US Marshals—nobody can seem to catch him. As a matter of fact, two of my best agents lost their lives in that explosion. I took action then. Hell! We all did. But for what? Lawson, it's like I'm fighting a fucking ghost here." He glared at me as I blew a bubble with my gum. "That's why I called you."

Goody sat back in his rugged leather seat and put on that clumsy smile he's so known for. And he's forever saying one thing while meaning another. Every time I come into this stankin' ass office, by the time I leave, I feel like I've been deluded. Bamboozled!

"You're being relocated to America," he announced.

"What?"

Just then, the door opened behind me, and two agents entered the room. One of them I recalled seeing…vaguely as my memory sprinted for recognition.

Goody reached into his pocket. He pulled out one of those god-awful, half-smoked stankin' cigars. He looked over the cigar and blew away a small amount of lint. Then he stuck the cigar in the corner of his mouth and continued. "Lawson, you're the best I've got, practically the best in the field if you ask me."

I sat there speechless, wanting to say more…

"You'll be reinstated in New York," he continued. "And these dashing young men will be more than happy to brief you."

Goody pulled out a match and struck it against his rugged, sandpaper-like beard. The match lit with ease. He took the cigar from his mouth, which he hadn't lit yet.

Thank God.

"Goody, I —"

Then he threw his hands up and yelled. "I stuck my neck out for you. And I did a lot of things that I shouldn't have done to pull the strings on the doll!"

The fire on his match began to die, and just before the flame simmered to an end, he lit his cigar, puffing quickly.

Goody coughed as he blew his smoke into the ceiling. "Canieya, there is no one here with a record like yours. Almost four hundred arrests. You got a vendetta, Lawson. That's why I chose you, and that's why everyone looks at you like that. They know, Lawson… They know!"

Then it hit me. Crane had already turned me into a monster. A beast. And I didn't even know it.

"Shit, I just hate it had to come to this," Goody mumbled as he sat back in his chair, blowing his horrid cigar smoke into the air.

While chewing my gum, I realized that I was this much closer to chopping off Vaydin's dick and shoving it in a blender, only to make him drink it. Nope! I'm not apologizing …

Just then, one of the agents spoke. "We've got everything covered," he asserted with a positive vibe.

"Your flight leaves tomorrow." Goody beamed as I nodded with a grin.

This could be fun…

CHAPTER: 10

Game Day

Rutherford, New Jersey
MetLife Stadium

My afternoon reeked of beer and popcorn while I strolled through the stadium's parking lot. Bratwursts, hot dogs, ribs, hamburgers, and steaks were all over the place. The sight of each grill made my mouth water. But not now, I was expecting something greater than food.

With a burning hunger for access, I approached the ticket counter. Then I literally ran to the club-level seating.

My pace slowed as I walked cautiously down the stairs. About four steps away from my aisle, I noticed the back of Quincy's head. He was sitting near the center of the row. My seat was to the left of his. But to his right… Ohhh… to his right, I saw…her.

Okani.

The beautiful grade of curls… It was that afro again.

She was here, sitting with her legs crossed.

My stomach dropped so hard. Plus, I forgot to brush my teeth. I didn't shave either. Oh well. This was happening regardless.

With my chest out and my abs clinched, I scooted down

the row to my seat. She grew more gorgeous with every step I took.

She didn't look at me at all, as she was so fashionably fixed on the football game.

She wore a black leather coat buttoned up to her chest area. The buttons were a glittery smoke gray. They sat flush with a black scarf tucked inside the collar of her jacket. She wore a pair of what I like to call booty shorts. They were black and form-fitting. She had on a pair of black fishnets and some black leather thigh-high, stiletto-heel boots. They had a pointed toe, and they were full of straps and buckles. This outfit gave her more of a gritty look.

Father Harmon stood as I approached my seat.

"Derrick!" he yelled, opening his arms for a hug.

"What's up, man?" I softly responded as he hugged me tight.

Plainly speaking, I don't do hugs. Fortunately, the hug was so fast that I didn't need to use my arms.

"Sit down. We're still in the first quarter," he said.

The hot dog vendor yelled from afar, "Hot dogs! Get your hot dogs here!"

"Which number is Corey?" I asked.

"Number 12." Quincy replied.

Suddenly, it hit me, like a speeding brick to the face.

It overwhelmed every smell in the stadium. Pretending as if she wasn't there was pointless. Her smell, it weakened me.

I wanted to do something, but I couldn't. Her presence held me. I was unresponsive and turned on at the same time.

Fuck, I thought to myself.

Then Quincy leaned in and whispered in my ear. "You wanna switch seats?" He snickered.

Slick ass was swift in his timing. He giggled a little more as he sat back into his seat.

As bad as I wanted to say yes, I had to lie to keep control. "Na… I'm good."

And right then, Okani stood up. And every man on the aisle repositioned themselves, including me.

We made her path clear and overt.

She exited to the left of the aisle, toward my direction.

I could feel her coming.

"Excuse me," she thrummed as she passed.

The moment lasted forever.

We immediately made eye contact, piercing into each other's souls. Her eyes were clean, and she didn't have on a single brush of makeup.

My breath shortened, and I briefly lost consciousness. I felt hypnotized as if I was being put under a trance. Was I being bewitched?

Her steps were so precise.

Her balance was insane.

Quincy leaned over to me again as Okani reached the end of the aisle.

"Go get her!" he said. "Now's the time."

But I developed every excuse I could think of to support my lack of initiative. "There ain't enough money in Fort Knox. I can't afford her," I bluntly stated.

The clergyman's eyes lit up. "First off, there *isn't* any money in Fort Knox. The aliens took it. And secondly, you think this is about money?"

"Yeah. I know her type, Q."

Father Harmon sat up in his seat while aiming to entice me to pursue her. Frankly, I was afraid of being let down or rejected. I know it sounds crazy, but I was too immersed in this love thing. I was cold-blooded, gutter, and, however, a hopeless romantic wrapped all up in one.

I was looking at the floor as my leg shook from my desire.

"You're right… You can't afford her," said Quincy as he slouched back into this seat. "But she can afford you."

I looked up to make eye contact with the clergyman. And

he was staring directly into my face, as though I was somehow foiling his plans. Time was passing so fast as I sat there contemplating my next move.

"Why do you think she got up, huh?" Father Harmon asked. "And she walked in your direction. She could've gone the other way."

Point taken.

"Give the ball to Dunlo!" shouted a fan from behind us.

Just then, the Giants hiked the ball. The quarterback bombed the pigskin right into the hands of the speed demon.

The crowd went wild as he bolted off in a mad sprint.

And that's when I made my decision. Before I could even stand to my feet, Corey had already run a touchdown.

The crowd went wild!

Apparently, Corey ran so fast that he left all the other players stationary.

"He moves like us," a lady whispered.

The speed demon was standing in the end zone when he took off his helmet and pointed directly at me.

I read his lips as he looked dead in my face and yelled, "Go fucking get her!"

I stood to my feet as the ref blew the whistle.

Without waiting a second more, I took off through the aisle and up the stairs.

In my dash for love, I heard the ref announce over the intercom, *'Unsportsmanlike conduct. Number 12. Fifteen-yard penalty!'*

The crowd exploded, booing in total revulsion.

At the top of the stairs, I entered the breezeway.

That smell hit me hard, stopping me dead in my tracks. As I exhaled, I opened my eyes to relaxation. Did I just walk into a massage parlor?

To my left was a herd of people carrying on in their various activities. The smell of popcorn returned with a vengeance, but her aroma wreaked a beautiful havoc.

"Sore ua jūbun ni anata nonagia o torimashita," a sweet and melodious voice commented.

To my immediate right, and in the corner next to the stairs, I saw her. The splendid…

Okani.

Her smell doubled with intensity.

She stood propped up against the wall with her arms folded just like her brother. I looked at the heart-melting sight of her with no words to follow.

"Hmm…" She smirked as she unfolded her arms and walked over to me seductively. Then she held out her hand.

"Koko ni. Watashitoisshoni arukimasu," she softly stated as I reached out for her hand.

It was so soft. It felt like I was carrying a tiny cloud. Man, I drifted off to paradise.

We had been walking for a while before she began speaking softly again.

"That language you're speaking, what is it?" I queried.

She looked into my eyes as she continued to walk slowly. My hands started sweating.

"It's Japanese…," she said.

"Nice. But I want to understand you."

"Sorekara watashi wa, eigo de hanasudeshou," she replied.

"My father's first wife was killed during a terrorist attack," she then continued. "Corey was just a baby then. The attack was sudden. You couldn't brace for it. She was shot with an assault rifle. The bullets tore her limbs from her body. My father grabbed Corey in his arms and took off running as fast as he could.

"One day he collapsed in front of a farmhouse and the owners took him and Corey in.

"They gave him about a week's supply of food in a duffel bag. As well as several bottles, diapers, and even some extra cash for his travels. He used to tell me about how he'd stop running at night just to feed Corey. And after that, he would take off running again as fast as he could. My father was strong and resilient. But he was only human. But Corey's mother… she was something else."

"He passed out near the outskirts of China. And that's when he met my mother. She was walking by a large mass of rubble when she felt my father's heart beating. The vibration was so strong that it sent tiny tremors through the ground. He told me that my mother found him holding Corey. His grip was so tight, she had to pry Corey from his arms." She giggled.

"If it hadn't been for my mother, none of us would be here today."

"Wait… Your father traveled over how many miles?" I asked.

"Over eight thousand miles."

"On foot?"

"On foot," she confirmed as we reached a concession stand. "My brother's life has always been fast paced. Popcorn?"

San Francisco, California
Alcatraz Island

The sun shined bright with seagulls sailing in the sky. Soft waves caressed the edge of the island as civilians went about their day.

The interior of Alcatraz held its rustic feel, with tarnished walls and waxed floors. As a tour commenced within this historical penitentiary, a fair-skinned man stood in front of Al Capone's cell.

He was old and skinny with black, shiny sleek hair. He had bright blue vacant eyes, thin lips, and a pointy nose. He wore a black shirt, with a black suit and tie and a pair of black polished loafers. A long black overcoat finished the old man's ensemble.

He stood with his hands in his pockets, glaring at the rugged cell as another man approached from behind. The old man lowered his head and asked, "What's in a nest?"

"An icebox," the man answered.

"Lt. Oni… you're late," the old man mumbled as he passed the officer an envelope.

"Iceberg Matony," Oni whispered as he took the envelope. "Got something for you."

Oni passed Matony a packet of papers. "What's this?" he asked.

"Something I leaked from Horace Vaydin."

Matony took the packet and skimmed through it briefly. "It's just names," the mobster grumbled as he glanced over at Oni. "This is a hit list…"

"Yea, and I highlighted two names… Just figured you wanted some get back for that Primosa sting."

Right then, Matony stopped searching through the packet. He smiled and grumbled, "Crane."

"Canieya too," Oni said as Matony passed him back the packet. "Vaydins' working with the Xaris. Some big-time guys with some crazy tech. They can find anybody and go anywhere in a matter of seconds."

"That fucking crackhead cost me over three million dollars," Matony noted as he tucked his hands back into the pockets of his overcoat.

"Hey, I know a man," Oni said. "Eyes are kinda weird, but he'd make it simple and sweet."

"Good. Pay Crane and that hoer a visit."

"Will do." Oni turned to leave.

"Oh, and Lieutenant…" Oni peered back over his shoulder as Matony sneered, "make him suffer."

CHAPTER: 11

The Poof!

Rutherford, New Jersey
MetLife Stadium

Me and Okani, walked back to our seats. And every now and then, we would peek over to each other. Our lustful eyes gleamed with joy until time clicked the game to an end. Of course, the Giants won. And by a tremendous lead.

Okani stayed behind to avoid the hustle and bustle while Father Quincy and I took our leave. By the time we reached the exit doors, I heard a voice scream, "Egh!"

Quincy and I turned, and there stood the speedster.

Once again, startled by his sudden arrival, we batted our eyes in amazement.

Corey stood up against the stadium walls with his arms folded as usual. This precipitous viewing was strange enough, but what was even odder was that Corey was already in his civilian clothing. Unlike Father Harmon, who still donned his clerical attire. Maybe they were the only clothes he had.

"Holy shit, man. Aren't you supposed to be in the locker room?" I asked.

"Man, guess who I just ran into?" he responded. "The owner of Green Bay. He just offered me twice as much to trade."

The speedster gazed off into the distance like some sort of hero.

"How'd you get out here so fast?" asked the clergyman.

"You know what I told him?" Corey retorted as he began to walk off.

The speedster was purposely ignoring our questions as though we already knew the answers. *And* he was walking off like we weren't in conversation. Or maybe he thought we would take off behind him. Whatever the case was, the speedster was still talking as if we were right beside him. "I told that fool I got nine kids to feed. Deez nuts! You damn right I'll trade that twelve." His dialogue was nothing but perplexing.

Quincy turned and looked at me. He was so confused, I almost burst out laughing. He then took off behind Corey.

"Ah man, this cat is fucked up," I mumbled to myself.

Suddenly, a sweet and seductive voice echoed, "Kon nani hayaka nolco shimasu?"

A mesmerizing smell whipped me to pudding. And even though I had built up a fair quota of resistance, my body rebelled. And I lost all sense of self-control.

Okani.

She was leaning against her car with her arms folded, filling the pose with so much sex appeal. "Where *you* going?" she asked as she looked up to me with those dreamy eyes.

My soul floated to the heavens. Then the speedster and Quincy approached from the left. Corey was still babbling on about something. "Things don't happen like that, Q…not in my life. I run up walls like people walk on the streets. Ya dig?"

"Do you, do everything fast?" Quincy gasped as we gathered by Okani's car.

"Sis!" yelled the speedster.

The two embraced each other with a hug that lasted for a few seconds. They had an odd way of saying things to each other without saying anything at all.

"Derrick? Right?" hollered the speedster as he looked over at me, pointing sternly at Quincy before pointing at me. "I'm having an after-party at the house. You two… You and Quincy are not invited," he emphasized with a smirk.

"Corey!" Okani hissed as she jokingly pushed him away. "Don't be rude."

"Big Q!" Corey shouted, glancing over to the clergyman, who only waved his hand with fatigue.

I finally came within arm's reach when Okani focused on my eyes.

Man, she was so gorgeous I could eat her up. She was just irresistible.

"What time y'all coming?" yelled Corey from the rear.

He had to be talking to Quincy because Okani and I were in our own universe. Our own little world.

"I can be there by nine," Quincy answered.

"Will nine work for you?" Okani asked, glancing at me.

"Good question," voiced the clergyman, peeping at me as well.

"Yeah, Derrick?" sassed the speedster.

I was smiling from ear to ear, feeling as if I was affiliated with something greater than a gang. "I gotta pick up Bookie, first."

"Okay…," Quincy replied.

Okani looked me in the eyes as Corey and Q carried on in conversation. She put her index finger over her mouthwatering lips. "SSsssshhhhhh…" She reached into her fancy coat pocket and pulled out a folded-up piece of paper. It looked old and possibly refurbished. "Beauty is in the eye of the beholder. So is art," she stated while handing me the paper.

Maybe it was an old love letter that she wrote. She probably thought about giving it to me, then she changed her mind, balled it up, and threw it in the trash. She probably changed her mind again and took it out the trash, unballed it and —

— I don't know.

But I quickly unraveled the item.

It was the picture Bookie had drawn. Okani taped it back together.

I looked deep into the kiddy rendering and it fueled my heart. "Thank you."

"All right, y'all. I gotta head out," Corey announced. "Some cats talkin' shit online. I gotta serve 'em up like a waiter. In Decatur!"

Here again, I was lost in translation. The speedster was incapable of holding a sound form of discourse.

"See you later." Okani giggled as she reached into her purse. She pulled out her keys as I nodded my head. Then I turned away, tucking the drawing into my coat.

Okani unlocked her car as I trekked happily into the sunset.

"Hey, sis!" yelled the speedster. "You mind dropping me off at the —"

This was strange, especially for the speedster. He had yet to finish his sentence and he talks in quandary, all the time. Okani hadn't responded. And I didn't hear her door opening or shutting, either. Plus, the clergyman walks heavy. I recognize his distinctive steps anywhere.

Were they all just looking at me, waiting for me to turn around and join in with their celebratory MO? Or could they all be wondering why I chose to leave so early? Maybe we were supposed to take a photo… Na. Something's wrong, I wondered as I turned around. And —

Poof! They were all gone…

This happened so fast it scared me shitless.

Her car was still there, but it had a translucent, neon glow.

Her keys dangled vibrantly from the keyhole. It was as if she had just let them go. I stood in amazement and fear, rubbing my hand through the greenish hue about the side of Okani's car.

On the ground, I discovered the same greenish hue had spread a few feet out from her car. With my nose I sniffed the air to see if I could locate Okani's delectable smell. That's when I ended up turning in circles, glimpsing back to her car again in bewilderment.

"What thaaa fuuuucckkkk…," I mumbled.

After taking Okani's keys from her car, I bolted off into the stadium and over to the ticket counter.

"Hey!" I yelled.

The lady at the desk sat up, looking alert.

"Have you seen a priest and a girl? A really exotic girl? And a running back? Ughhh…" I stuttered and shook nervously.

The lady shook her head moronically, sitting back in a relaxed fashion. She smacked and popped away on her chewing gum, shuffling it about in her mouth. She crossed her legs and snickered, shaking her head again. "Sir? Really…? Do you know how many people I've seen today?"

"I mean, the running back. Ughhh… the Corey Dunlo guy. He plays for this team. The Giants!" I yelled.

"Sir! I don't know anything about football. I don't know what a first down is. I ring up tickets, and I answer the phone. I just work here. Right here. At *this* booth. Now, if you want to file a missing persons case, then you at the wrong desk, honey!" she wretchedly announced.

"Aggghhh!!!" I grimly growled, reaching for my cell phone.

"Don't get mad at me!" she blurted as I whirled around from the counter, piercing through the crowd.

Everyone else around this occurrence functioned as if they hadn't seen a thing. But I had Quincy on speed dial. The operator answered with her well-studied reply.

"We're sorry. But this number is no longer in service. Goodbye."

I called again.

"We're sorr—"

Click!

For a moment I stood still as the pedestrians passed. The stadium was nearly empty, and I had to get back to Bookie.

Maybe I should text him. But Quincy don't know how to text. By this time, my phone had nearly died. The unexplainable had shaped my day into a messy Rubik's Cube.

No one just evaporates into thin air.

Finally, I took off for my car. And eventually I made it back home.

But I had yet to understand what I saw. Then there was the fact that I still had Okani's keys.

As I approached my neighbor's house to pick up Bookie, I felt like I could tell Tom what happened, and he probably wouldn't look at me like I was crazy.

Walking cautiously up to his front door, I stood for a minute to gather myself. Just as I started to knock, the door swung open.

"Daddy! What can I do you for?" Bookie shouted, holding the door open.

"Hey, Mr. Derrick!" Tela shouted as Tom popped up behind his daughter.

"Man, we were just watching the news," Tom said. "How you doing?"

"Tom? I need your help, man…," I replied.

Tom looked around and back into his house before he stepped onto his porch. "Give us a minute, you two."

"Okay," Bookie whined.

"Tela and Bookie been playing and eating all day. You seen Dunlo? Man, that guy is unnatural." Tom then shut the door softly behind him. "What's up, bro?"

"I got to tell you something."

"Okayyyy…"

"Promise me you won't get all crazy on me?"

"Scout's honor," he replied. He then folded his arms and put his back against the door.

"So, I went to the football game today. And Okani was there —"

"-Your girlfriend?"

"Yeah. I mean, no. Not yet," I stammered. "To make a long story short. We were all standing outside, right? Quincy, the Dunlos, and myself."

"Uh-huh. Wait! You know Corey Dunlo?"

"Yes! But I was talking to Okani, and we decided to get together later. Something about an after-party at Corey's house."

"And you need a condom," Tom advised as he relaxed.

"They're gone, Tom. All of them," I said.

"Oh. I see…," he muttered.

"No, Tom…you don't get it. I was walking to my car. And

within a few seconds, I turned around, and *poof*! All of them were gone."

"That's odd," he said.

I just knew Tom didn't believe me. I expected him to start laughing.

"Okani's keys were still jingling from the car door," I firmly stated.

Tom got quiet.

"It was like she let them go." I took her keys out of my pocket. My eyes watered up as I tossed them over to Tom.

He caught them with a sudden jolt.

"Tom… I'm not crazy, man. I know what I saw."

"I've heard of this same type of thing happening to random people," he said. "It was, like, one minute they were there, the next minute, they weren't… Were there any clothes left behind?"

"No. But there was this odd neon-colored hue on her car and on the ground where they were standing."

Tom looked at the keys for a second. "So, what…? Are these her keys?"

"Yeah. I need you to come with me to get her car, so it

doesn't get towed. Please?"

My lips began to tremble. I was sad, but Tom was a true friend. He stared at me and shut his eyes tight. He breathed in and bumped his head against the door behind him. He exhaled and opened his eyes, gazing at me with a capricious look.

"Give me a second," he said as he opened the door. He slowly and calmly walked back into his house.

Tom had taken the keys with him. He left his front door wide open as I waited on the porch. And Bookie was just staring at me through the screen door.

"Hey, Derrick!" Tom yelled from the living room.

"Yeah?"

"Come in here."

This was my first time stepping in Tom's house. I felt kind of strange and out of place as I entered with care, closing the door behind me.

"Daddy!" Bookie shouted as I entered. She wrapped herself around my leg as I glanced over Tom's house.

Everything was so in order and tidy. His living room was to my left. He stood in front of a gorgeous couch watching the news on a large flat-screen TV, mounted perfectly on the wall, just above a massive fireplace.

His wife, Vera, sat on the couch watching the news as well and without even admonishing my entrance. She didn't even turn around to see who I was.

Then I overheard the news anchor talking about the football game. Just then, I stepped closer to Tom's side as the anchorman delivered his findings. I tried to make eye contact with his wife, to speak with her in some type of way. And that's when they showed a clip of Okani's car.

"There! That's her car! You see it!" I shouted.

Suddenly, Tom's wife glared at me with a blank gaze.

"We're going!" Tom firmly stated. "I'll be right back, hun."

"Can I come?" Bookie asked.

"… Bookie, stay here with me," Tela said. "We can play pillow fort in my room."

Vera turned off the TV with the remote she had been holding from the moment of my entrance. She turned around, quite creepy in style, to stare at me again.

This woman was fierce, and she didn't look American at all. We instantly sized each other up the minute we made eye contact.

"And what's the plan?" she asked with a Russian accent.

"We gotta get the car back to her house," Tom added.

She stood to her feet and pulled out her cell phone while

still staring into my eyes.

Vera was taller than Tom and built like an Amazon.

"What's her name?" she asked while still looking me in my eyes.

"Hun?" Tom muttered.

"Okani Dunlo," I quietly commented.

Vera started dialing into her phone without looking at the numbers. She was still intently studying my every action. She then stomped off into the rear of the house as the phone dialed. What was even stranger was that she was walking backwards, still watching me as she exited the living room.

"We don't have time for this. Bookie can stay here with Tela. Let's go, man!" Tom yelled.

He bolted off for the front door and I followed. And so did that atypical or freakishly snide greeting from his wife.

Something wasn't right about her.

Minutes later, we pulled back into the stadium's parking lot. The ride would've normally taken about an hour, but I was flying through red lights and stop signs. I must've been going a hundred. I was just so pumped and psyched up that I didn't notice.

Everybody was gone. The news crew and the football players.

Tom and I got out of the car simultaneously. I crept over

to the area where Okani had parked.

"What the hell?" I yelled.

"What?" Tom retorted.

"Her car! It's gone! It was right here. I was right there, and she was parked right over here," I explained. "Fuck, man!"

"Is that it?" asked Tom while pointing to the ground.

"Yes…" I replied, focusing on the discolored circle. The color was a bit duller. In fact, it had nearly vanished.

"Man, that's pretty faint."

"Something ain't right, Tommy G," I responded.

"I believe you. Man, this is going to sound wild, but I think it's the government. They be testing shit on people all the time. It's either them or…" He paused for a minute as he studied the coloration. "…Aliens."

My quest for the truth about aliens had waxed cold. Maybe because I wanted too much, and my wants outweighed that idle alien fancy.

Tom got so engulfed in this that he laid on the ground.

"Tom?" I quietly asked as he positioned himself dead center of the discoloration. "What are you doing, man?"

Tom didn't respond. He just hummed like he enjoyed

what he was doing. "Aaannnddd… Bingo!" he hollered while pointing to the sky.

"Bingo? What bingo?!"

Tom was winking his eye, trailing his finger to an exact point in space. "That's the answer, man... Yep!" he shouted confidently as he got up from the ground.

"Okay…" I shook my head in confusion.

"Aliens, man! … Look," he whispered, pointing to the sky.

My eyes followed his finger up slowly.

"You see that?" he asked as I peered upward, trying to figure out what he was seeing.

But then I saw the clouds. They formed a perfectly shaped doughnut. The inner circle was large and clear of aerial vapors. The clouds that made up the outer ring were all turning in various directions, gelled together in a massive formation. It was noticeably wide but flowy, like an attenuated spread of fog. The cloudy doughnut appeared to be just as transparent as the neon discoloration on the ground. But the inside of the doughnut looked like a hole.

The setting grew sinister.

"Theoretically, we are looking into a portal," Tom explained. "A doorway of some sort. I don't know if it's the entrance or the exit, or both."

"Are they done?" I asked, peering into the circular hole.

"I've never seen anything like this," Tom whispered.

Suddenly, the cloudy ring vanished.

"Let's get out of here," I suggested.

"Damn right!" Tom bellowed as we dashed to the car. This could've just been a feeling but it felt like we were being chased by the X-Files.

When we got back home, it was early in the a.m. He and I were both troubled and chilled by the sighting. We hadn't spoke since we left the stadium.

I pulled up to Tom's driveway as he stared over to my house. "I'll get Bookie for you," Tom nervously stated. He took Okani's keys out of his pocket and handed them to me. "Maybe all this talk about aliens is just smoke in mirrors, y'know?"

"You think so?" I asked as Tom opened the car door.

"Maybe… But that still doesn't explain those clouds… moving like that." he responded as he pulled the door back a tad. "That shit's unacceptable. Well, I got to get in, man. We'll figure this out." He yawned as he opened the door again.

With a jumbled face, I sat there, gawking straight ahead as Tom shut the door.

"Something's bound to turn up." He said as I rolled down

my window.

Just when Tom reached the porch, his wife yanked the front door open. She pushed Bookie out and snatched Tom in.

"Thanks, Tom!" I yelled.

"Yep!" he hollered as Bookie skipped down the driveway.

Instead of Bookie getting in the car, she skipped on over to the house.

After parking, I got out of the car and I opened my squeaky front door.

"I'm sleepy, Daddy," Bookie moaned.

"Okay, Bookie. Go put on your night clothes."

As she headed to her room, I shut the front door and locked it. I tossed Okani's keys on the kitchen counter. For a solid thirty minutes I stared into the kitchen. Then, I taped Bookie's drawing to the refrigerator door.

Devastated by the happenings, I finally collapsed on the couch in front of the living room window. Sitting with my knees in the cushions, I held the blinds open, and I watched the sky like a hawk…

CHAPTER: 12

Gateways

August 8, 2025
Queens, New York: LaGuardia
7:00 a.m.

On the way to baggage claim, my two compadres finally decided to introduce themselves.

"I'm Agent Woods, and this is Agent Lockley," Woods informed as he gestured to the man beside him.

After shaking Wood's hand, my fuzzy recollection of him sparked again. "Haven't I seen you before?"

"About two years ago I visited the SIS headquarters in London to meet with Chief Goodrum."

"Ohhhww! You were the guy waiting by his office."

"Yea," Woods muttered just as Agent Lockley approached.

"Agent Lawson, I want you to understand that you are now part of an elite team," Lockley noted. "So many people just became your enemy. And no matter what happens, you have to keep your head on straight."

"That sounds like my old job," I replied as Agent Woods grabbed all the bags.

Woods was about six feet tall, and if my memory serves me right, the last time I saw him, he was a bit thinner than Lockley. But now, Agent Wood's was a hunk! He had a wide face, a rough beard, and a buzz haircut. His eyes were blue, and his nose was big and stubby.

He walked over to me as we stood near the baggage claim.

"We are looking for a man with a rap sheet from here back to the plane we just got off," he bellowed, way louder than necessary.

"My ex!" I shouted.

"I assure you, ma'am, this is no joking matter. Being a kick-ass agent isn't half of it. You must be vigilant," Lockley proclaimed. "Vaydin has a group of followers. Assassins that move with the shadows."

I was blown away, thinking that I had gone mad. "So, I don't need my eyes checked?"

Lockley glanced away in disappointment. With his head down, he sighed as if he expected me to be another way. Lockley was a bit skinnier and about a foot shorter than Woods. He had blond spiky hair and his face was clean as a baby's bottom. His eyes were light green, and his nose was small. He had a straight chin and a strong jawline. His cheekbones were well defined, and his lips were thin. He looked like he walked out of an Axe commercial. But they both wore all black tactical vests, Chalker slings, gloves, and combat boots.

"We don't know much about them, but we do believe that they have been working with Vaydin for quite some time," Woods explained.

We made it through the metal detectors, and Agent Woods stopped to speak with the airport staff.

"I'm grabbing coffee," I said while searching over my pockets. "You want something?"

"Yea," Lockley replied. "Two sugars and a lot of cream."

About five minutes later, I reached the coffee stand.

"Nice coat," the barista complimented. "What can I get you?"

Now I felt a bit sexy wearing my black snakeskin leather coat, a black shirt, a pair of thigh-high boots, and my favorite pair of black leather leggings. "Thanks." I mumbled as I pinned up my hair with my weaponized hair clamp. The retractable razor is so incognito that I forget I'm wearing it. "Let me get two cups. One black and one with two sugars and a lot of cream."

"Condiments are in the baskets to your left."

"Oh sweet. I didn't see that."

My eyes fixed ahead as the barista sat the cups on the bar. Then he slowly backed away with his hands raised.

Carefully, I peered over my shoulder to view a bright window of light opening out of thin air. My eyes blinked with suspicion as three hoodlums stepped through this window. Then, the gateway closed.

Clk-Chk!

"Great." I whispered… as a 9mm grazed against my temple.

The Bronx, New York:
Crane's Residence

Lying in bed with my eyes wide open, I pondered over the strange disappearance of Quincy and the Dunlos. Yesterday was the weirdest day ever. Just then, Bookie burst into my room.

Bboom!

"Daddy, Daddy! Can we have cereal for breakfast?" she hollered.

"Great Scott, Bookie! It's… What time is it?" I wondered.

"I don't know," she said while settling next to me.

I rolled in the opposite direction to notice the alarm clock. "Bookie, it's seven in the morning,"

"That's a good time, Daddy," she said. "Cartoons come on in about another hour. It's gonna take you forty-five minutes to get up. If you get up now, we'll have fifteen minutes to get some cereal and sit down for the morning's lineup."

At this moment, I sat straight up in the bed, shocked at such a timed stratagem. Bookie was not your average five-year-old. I knew I was training her to be smarter and wiser than the norm, but she excelled fast. She was monstrously brainy.

"You're right," I mumbled.

She jumped on the bed and wrapped her arms around my neck. "C'mon, Daddy!" she pleaded.

I sighed from the lag of morning rest. "Okay, okay… Give me a minute."

"Forty-five minutes Daddy," informed the smart child as she smiled away.

She freed her grip and bounced about the bed a few times before leaping to the floor. "I'm gonna brush my teeth, Daddy!" she hollered while running out of the room.

Queens, New York: LaGuardia

"Where's Crane?" a voice mumbled.

"Who the hell is that?" I answered as my hands lifted in the air.

Blam!

The man fired, but I had already slammed him to the ground with an ippon seoi-nage.

"Aaaagggghhhh!!!" he yelled in traumatic anguish as I broke his wrist, flicking the gun away.

LaGuardia turned into a war zone when another gangster opened fire.

I rolled out of dodge and over to a newsstand. The hoodlums darting after me.

Screams echoed as the gangster grabbed me by the collar.

I roundhouse-kicked him in the face and snatched his gun away, ejecting the magazine. I swept him to the ground and aimed; squeezing the trigger, the bullet jammed.

Tossing the gun away, I dug my knees into the gangster's chest, seizing the razor from my hair.

Ssicszh!

I slashed through his neck, splashing blood to the floor.

Fastening the clip back into my hair, I spun around, striking into a bony gangster.

He stumbled back as the bulky thug opened fire.

I bowled up to the coffee stand, clutched up a cup of coffee, and threw it in in face.

Skiishh!

"AAAAgaggaghhhh!!!" he bellowed, firing blindly.

As the bony gangster charged with various punches, I tumbled over and kicked him in the face.

He grabbed me with a bear hug, circling me around.

I drop-kicked the bulky goon, knocking his gun to the floor.

Sinking my stance out of the bear hug, I gripped the vandal's wrist with my hands and slid between his legs.

With an inverted seoi-otoshi, I stood, flipping him over my shoulder.

Bllooom!

He slammed to the ground.

I bowled over him and toward the bulky thug as he grabbed his gun.

While clearing his line of sight, I windmill-kicked the gun from his hand. My second kick plastered him to the floor.

Bish!!

The bony gangster rushed me with a series of punches.

I countered, jabbed, and spun with a front kick to the head.

Cram!

I snatched the clamp from my hair and diced through his neck.

Skittts!!

Blumf!

He hit the floor while the bulky thug squinted for clarity. As he reached for his gun, several officers entered the scene.

I juggled the razor clip over and sprinted into a roundoff.

He fired in error as I somersaulted into a swan dive. Spreading my arms, I swished through his neck.

Shissssh!

Blood spritzed into my face like a sprinkler as I belly-flopped, rolling quickly to my feet. I fixed the clamp back into my hair while the carnage spilled from his jugular.

The bitch failed as he plopped to the floor.

Ranting at the zenith of discomfort was the ringleader, laying only a few feet away. He reached for his gun. But before he could seize the weapon, I skipped into a roundoff and a backward salto.

The aerial's momentum planted my foot precisely… fracturing his other wrist.

Skcugm!

"Aaaagggghhhh!!! You fucking bitch!" he screamed as I turned him over to his back, plonking my knees in his chest.

Flipping his gun in the air, I caught the grip upended, and scraped the slide over the ground, cocking the bullet into the chamber. The motion ended with the barrel thrusting violently into his temple.

"Drop the gun!" an officer shouted.

"MI-6!" Woods replied as he approached with his badge. "She's with us!"

The Bronx, New York:
Crane's Residence

With a shaky hand, I poured the milk over Bookie's cereal. "Here," I mumbled while passing her the bowl.

She looked up at me with those sparkling eyes and shouted, "Thank you, Daddy!"

It was three minutes to eight when she carefully walked to the living room. She sat her bowl on the table in front of her. Then she picked up the remote and turned on the television.

"I love you, Daddy!" Bookie yelled as she tuned to her

favorite station. She hadn't looked away at all.

This little girl had done the impossible and I could only watch with amazement. She cured me of my criminal nature, and I had forgiven all of my past adversaries.

In a sense, karma had looked over me. Every time I looked into her big brown eyes; I grasped a piece of redemption.

Right then, I looked back to my old refrigerator. I found myself staring at it as my thoughts took me away.

For a second there, I forgot about all of the crimes I committed. All I could think about was Okani, the strange disappearance, and my dispersed idea of a family. My heart was prepared to move on from Canieya. I wasn't sure if she wanted to communicate or not.

Was she still angry with me? Or was this all a safety precaution?

"Daddy! You gonna watch cartoons with me?" Bookie asked, snapping me out of my daze.

She was standing up on the couch, still chewing, with milk running down the side of her mouth.

"Aaaahhh… Why not?" I answered.

I got up from the kitchen table and walked over to the

living room.

She plopped down in the seat and wrapped herself up in a blanket. "Where's yo' cereal at, Daddy?" she asked as she carefully grabbed her bowl up from the table in front of her.

"Oh, Ima just pick out of yours," I joked.

"Nuh-uh! These my cereals!" Then she thought about it and held out one kernel. "Okay, Daddy. You can have one."

"One cereal? What's that go do?" I chuckled out loud.

I gravitated back into the kitchen and sat in my seat, staring at Okani's keys and the refrigerator, again.

There was nothing special about the refrigerator. Well, Tom gave it to me a long time ago. But it was my thoughts. My thoughts had consumed me greatly.

I had yet to understand why the police hadn't come to interrogate me about the disappearance of Quincy and the Dunlos.

I mean, I knew Lawson created new lives for us, new identities. But how long? How long would this web of lies last? How long would this life prevail in the wake of justice?

Just then, Bookie burst into the kitchen full of energy. "Daddy!"

"Yes, baby?"

She walked over to the table and pulled out her chair at the opposite end. With her blanket in hand, she grunted and scuffled into the chair. Finally, she settled in her seat and huffed,

"Whew! Mommy's not coming, is she?"

"No, Bookie. She's not coming."

"Do you know why, Daddy? Is she mad at you?" she asked while kicking her legs about.

"Baby, Daddy don't know. Honestly, she's probably never coming back," I softly mumbled.

We both sat back in our seats, and at the same time.

A complete silence entered the room. And for a minute, I drifted off in thought.

"Daddy, let's go outside and play!" Bookie insisted.

Now that's an idea. Hopefully, this would shake loose the cobwebs in my head. "Sounds good, Bookie! Let's do it!"

"Yay! I'll go get my ball!" She climbed down out of her chair and dashed off to her room.

I waited patiently, staring at the refrigerator again. Maybe the white color and the various child drawings gave me a calming spirit that allowed my mind to wander. But I just couldn't put the situation together. How in the world did Quincy and the Dunlos vanish?

Then thoughts of Canieya raced through my head. My desire to call her bugged me until I retrieved my phone from my pocket. Our family, this odd unity, had backed me into a corner. But I'm no loser. And I vowed to never ever go back to my criminal mind. Plus, Bookie deserved a better way of living. And that's when I pressed the power button. The phone didn't do a damn thing.

"I found it, Daddy!" Bookie yelled from the rear of the house, once again snapping me back to reality. "I went ahead and changed clothes, too," she added.

Bookie hurried over to the table as I connected my phone up to the charger plugged in the socket by the fridge. Finally, I looked down to my side as she approached with a smile.

"You ready, Daddy?"

She always asks that.

"Yeah. Let me grab my shoes." As I walked over to the door to get my shoes, I reminded her, "Now we go have to play in the front, 'cause we aint got no backyard."

"I know Daddy. And we gotta stay out the street, too."

"Yes. How'd you know I was gonna say that?"

"You always do, Daddy. Let's play kickball!" she then screamed.

With a smile, I opened the front door and pondered. "How we go play kickball with just two people?"

"You can roll the ball to me, and I'll kick it," she briefly replied. "So, then you gotta catch it and tag me out, Daddy!"

"Alright, but I'm not taking it easy on you," I inserted.

She giggled and jumped with energy as she held onto her beloved red ball.

We needed this.

The sun rose as we ganged up in the front yard. Bookie was making bases for our little game of kickball. She grabbed a stick for first base. Then she found a larger stick for second base, a small, old, and damaged Styrofoam cup for third base, and her little plastic red chair for home base.

"All right, Bookie. Now how we go do this?" I asked. And that's only because she had all the answers.

She shrugged. "I don't know, Daddy. Oh wait! Let's say I make it to first base, right?"

"Uh-huh…"

"Then we put a ghost man on first base," she explained.

I giggled. "Ghost man? Naw…I don't like the sound of that."

"DAdddyyyyy??"

"Okay. Okay… I was just kidding. Ghost man on first. Gotcha!"

"Then I have to kick again," she continued.

"All I have to do is step on second base to tag out your ghost man."

"No, Daddy, that won't be fair. I have to run from home straight to second base to put a ghost man there," she explained.

"Oh…" I nodded. "We do that for all the bases?"

"Yep! Now let's play!" she screamed while jumping around.

This approach to the game of kickball made absolutely no sense. Be that as it may, the conclusion didn't help nor hinder her excitement. The aim here was just to have fun, simply stated.

She stood in front of her little red chair as I backed to the edge of our yard.

"Okay, Bookie, it's coming fast!" I shouted while preparing my pitch.

She breathed hard, blowing air in and out, as if she was getting ready to sprint. "Let's go…," she mumbled while shaking her hands hysterically.

That's when I pitched the ball.

She sprinted from the chair, kicking as hard as she could.

Biff!

"Whoa!" I yelled.

The ball rolled off toward the street. I ran to retrieve the ball and when I turned around, she was standing on first base.

"Ghost man on first!" she hollered as she skipped back to

her little red chair.

"I would believe so…"

"Don't take it easy on me, Daddy," she ordered as I walked back to my alleged pitching mound.

Who the hell does she think I am?

"Oh no! Not today," I replied as she jumped up and down shaking her hands in lively, fervent motions. This girl was destined to win. And from the very first play of the game our aggressive tendencies bubbled, like a shook can of soda. Bookie took after me. And to a great extent.

For a minute there, I thought this was just kickball, but Nnaaaaaa… Fuck that.

It's game time.

I pitched the ball twice as hard. She darted from her plastic chair, sprinting like an athlete off the blocks.

Biff!

She kicked the ball clean into the sky.

I squinted into the blinding sun as the gusty winds captured the ball and sent it over my head. "Shit!" I shouted, dashing off to fetch the ball.

"Ooohww…Daddy…You said a bad word!" Bookie said

as the ball rolled into the neighbor's yard, and between the houses' alley. "That's a free point." She yelled from afar.

I didn't care. As far as I was concerned, the play was still good. Plus, I didn't know if she was still running the bases.

Who the hell said she could go first anyway?

The ball had almost rolled under the back porch as I darted into the house alley. All I could think about was how hard I would bean her across the head for humiliating me.

After snatching up the ball, I whirled around and dashed back to the front yard.

As I turned the corner, I was blinded by a light. Now, it couldn't have been the sun; because the sun was rising behind me.

I couldn't rightly perceive the fortuity that odiously installed itself into my slate of time. Never did I expect such an act of misfortune. My nerves ended abruptly. Now there was no need for puzzling questions.

Canieya was too late for this one…

The sun shinned indeed, but my front yard had become too dark, inky, and blistering to my visual concept. The search for amusement cleared itself from this morning's database.

On a side note, the universe speaks in volumes, and sometimes, it speaks in volumes that we may never store. Why?

Well, maybe because the magnitude is way too substantial to understand in its entirety. But I understood this. And at the same time, I suffered from a misconstrued cessation. My plans, her plans, the neighbor's plans… everybody's plans ceased in significance. Cause I know major. And this was beyond major.

So… who am I? Really?

What was my purpose? Or what was my value?

How much would become too much for mental consumption?

Would we collapse from the shock of horrific sightings?

At this moment, I was far from any of these. Instead, I invited death. And for a variety of reasons...

One, I couldn't beat this, unfurling horror.

Two, Canieya would never forgive me for such a loss, a juggernaut in unimaginable weight.

And three, I had finally failed. Totally.

If I didn't act fast, my life would take a turn for the worse.

Mortally wounded and socially convicted, my past evils caught up with me, lastly seizing my soul.

I easily hated myself as I kneeled petrified, stiff as a freezing glacier. I couldn't blink, think or sink any lower. I was too far away, and my adrenaline escaped me for the first time.

If I had only eaten some cereal and watched cartoons a

little while longer. Maybe staying inside would've thwarted the event at hand. Well, I don't know… When somebody wants you bad enough, they'll find you. Not even protective custody could obstruct a constructed death.

Yet and still, I had done too much.

I wronged so many people, regardless of my reasoning. And in my quest to redeem myself, I helped Canieya bring in so many fugitives. But she didn't do anything to anyone. Not like I did.

Could it be?

My objectives colliding with my past objections.

And here I was, thinking karma ignored my criminal endeavors. I was such a fool—silly me. No one supersedes karma. No one…

Damn my life. Fuck it all to hell!

I quivered away as I came to grips with this sudden arrangement. My eyes traveled from the ground, trapping the sight of an evil and uncivil substance of a man.

A man that I've never seen before, stood boldly in my front yard.

He wore some all-black combat boots, some dark fatigue pants with a black wife beater tucked in, a black utility belt and a large black overcoat, full of pockets. With the coat's collar popped, he covered a great portion of his slender face.

He had dark skin with small lips, and a big nose. He was tall with brown dreads hanging down his back.

His eyes were soulless, audaciously tormenting evil.

He clenched Bookie by her throat with one hand.

Then, holding a chrome 357 Magnum in his other hand, he skimmed lightly against her tender temple.

This was all happening as soon as I turned the corner, after chasing down her red ball.

The dread-headed reprobate didn't even give me time to speak.

He pulled the trigger quickly.

Blam!

And just like that, I watched helplessly as my Bookie's head blew off into fragments.

He threw her body to the ground like a trash bag, and he walked off into a window of light...

I wanted to follow the scoundrel, but I couldn't. Because the doorway closed, leaving me utterly too sick to stand.

I left my gun, and my criminal mind in the house. But the neighborhood responded fast. And at this moment, no one cared about what color I was or how I was dressed. All they knew was that Bookie was dead.

They came out of their homes running at full speed. I couldn't look in their eyes, for self-guilt ravaged my mind. But I could hear them screaming.

From across the street, Tom peeked through his blinds. "Bookie! Oh no, Bookie!" He screamed as he sprinted across the street with his cell phone.

He shuffled in the grass, collapsing weightlessly to the ground beside me.

"Oh man…no… Jesus help us," he cried.

I dropped the ball and crawled over to Bookie's corpse as her blood painted the grass purple.

Ms. Vivian and Carl from across the way came jogging down the street. So many conversations filled the air, and I couldn't hold back my despondent sobbing.

I reached out for my Bookie and held her close to me. While sitting on my knees, I stared at the wound that used to be her head. Blood was everywhere. It soaked my clothes instantly.

Everyone crowded around me.

Tom clenched his hands into my shoulders. My body shook and jolted, as if I was being electrocuted by anguish.

Tom wrapped his arm around my shoulder and rocked me back and forth. From left to right, I swayed as he mumbled a prayer. And that's when it happened. My crying intensified until I just resorted to screaming. The pain of all my evils visited me with open arms. All of my wrongs, my hundreds of enemies, began to manifest.

That gunshot had yet to settle. The sound would forever echo though my head. Forever, will it rocket through my soul.

My neighbors began to cry as I eyed the sky, screaming without ceasing.

My Bookie. My only child.

Sirens wailed, but at the same time, I heard nothing.

Then, I suddenly stopped crying. The tears, snot, and sobbing ceased as my anger increased. My criminal mind returned with a vile showering of hatred, a sun dance of explosive antipathy. I looked straight into nothing, clearly gazing through anyone who stood in front of me.

My facial expression turned into a blank canvas as I gripped Bookie tighter.

The sirens blared on as the Ambulance finally approached the edge of my driveway. I hadn't moved an inch and neither had Tom. A few of my neighbors were still lurking, speaking frantically to each other. But I had been rendered speechless.

As my memory recycled, I bit into my bottom lip until it

bled. His face was as clear as day. And I never forget a face… Never.

Queens, New York: LaGuardia

After the officers finished cleaning the scene and dispersing the crowd, Agent Woods and Lockley muttered among themselves. I strolled over, wiping the blood from my face.

"What the hell were you guys doing, playing with action figures?" I queried, walking over to Woods as several other officers scuttled about.

"Goodrum told me you were good, but he didn't say you were *that* good," Woods asserted as he reached into his coat pocket. He gave me a handkerchief and an ID card. "Here," he added with reverence.

Lockley gawked with anger as he pointed with discord. "You're intolerable. Foolish. Your aggression, lack of structure, and stability will cost you your life. You and your actions are not acceptable. Furthermore, I can't allow you to insist on such unpredictable impulses."

"Yeah, I take some getting used to," I declared as I took the handkerchief from Woods.

"Oh yeah? I don't get used to you. *You* get used to *me*!" he insisted as I walked away with self-admiration.

Then suddenly, I froze in my steps. It felt like I lost

something. Something important…

“Lawson?” Agent Woods asked as he approached my side. “Hey, you okay?”

My heart dropped into my stomach as I propped myself up on the wall. “I’m fine… Just a little lightheaded.”

Then my cell phone rang…

The Bronx, New York: Montefiore Medical

"Mr. Lawson!"

I turned around, looking back into the waiting lobby to see the officer holding the phone between his face and shoulder. "Sir! I got your wife on the phone now," the officer noted with delight. "Would you like me to break the news or…?"

He looked puzzled as I shook my head. Only because Canieya was in London, and there was no way she could make it to New York within a decent amount of time. "Is she on hold?" I whispered.

"Ughhh… kinda," he inserted.

"Tell her that her mom was in a car wreck."

The officer looked confused again as he held the phone still.

"Please… I'll tell her," I mumbled. "If she comes."

The officer nodded. Then, a look of gloom came over him as he hung the phone up. "Sir, your wife is on the way."

I whirled around, looking at him with a stroke of disbelief. "What?" I howled from the empty bellows of my soul.

"She landed at LaGuardia about an hour ago," he added.

What type of devil-witch timing is this?

For sure, I thought she was still in London. But I knew I had to tell her the truth. The walls closed in as I grabbed my chest.

My breaths grew short.

"Sir," the officer shouted as he hung up the phone.

The officer made his way over to me as I propped my hands up on my knees and glared into the shiny, newly waxed floor. My reflection was pitiful. But a glow of hatred covered me when I recalled the hand-drawn portrait of Bookie's assailant. One of the NYPD artists rendered the image before I came to the hospital, and I kept it tucked away in my coat pocket. The thought of him made my eye twitch with an intense gust of loathing.

The officer stumbled as he drew closer. He reached into his top shirt pocket and pulled out a bunch of folded tissues. "Was she your first child?" he asked while handing me a tissue.

"My only child," I replied as I politely took the tissue. "I need some air." I spoke, stumbling through the sliding door and into the night's sky.

The officer followed me out, saying, "Man, I couldn't imagine that feeling. I don't have any kids, but I do have a brother." He said as he stood next to me with his back against the wall. "He's been going in and out of a coma for about a year now. Every time he goes off into that...sleep, I feel like dying.".

"Me too," I interjected.

Then, in the distance, I saw Tom walking from his car.

I couldn't hold it anymore. I started weeping all over again.

"You okay, homie?" Tom asked as he approached.

I sniffed while answering. "I'm holding on. I got an image of the murdered drawn. And… Canieya's coming."

"Damn," he grumbled. Tom reached into his coat, and pulled out a card. "This is from us. Vera's idea."

"Thanks, Tommy G," I replied with a smirk as I stuffed the card into my back pocket.

"Anytime, homie." Tom said as he walked off. He entered the hospital and sat in the lobby.

The officer pulled out a cigarette and he lit it with a small lighter. As I sat on the curb, gazing off into nothing, the officer stared up into the sky…

An hour passed when I found myself, pacing back and forth, right outside the door of the freezing morgue. I was so angry, sad, and mixed up. I propped up against the wall.

Then I heard it—the voice of all voices.

"What the hell are we doing down here?" Canieya shouted from outside the main hallway doors.

I knew it was her. I'd recognize that vocal vent anywhere.

Suddenly, the hallway doors swung open, and two brutes wearing some form of military gear walked in. I immediately glared into their faces to make sure they didn't fit the mental description of Bookie's killer that was plastered to my brain.

The agents weren't moving fast enough for me to see her. Or maybe I was a bit too anxious. I don't know. Maybe I wasn't ready to see her. But I couldn't leave now… I had to face her.

Bookie had been saving me for so many years. But now, not even she, in this aftermath, could save me from Canieya's wrath. I could feel the floor shaking as she shoved the double doors open.

She made her grand entrance, and I saw her clearly as we made eye contact.

She stopped in her footsteps. Her eyes wandered rampantly.

She almost turned around, but I quickly opened the door to the morgue.

She paused as I held the doors open.

The two liaisons walked up to me. "Mr. Lawson. I'm Agent Woods," one said as he shook my hand.

He stepped aside, and the other agent entered the morgue without a greeting. I didn't care because I was still looking at Canieya.

She continued to damage me with her stern look.

Crumbling to the floor, I burst into tears and balled up against the wall. I could feel her standing over me with a face of dominating pity.

"Did I miss something here?" Woods asked from afar.

"Derrick?" Canieya whispered. "What the hell's going on here, *Derrick*? I just landed not too long ago. Saw yo' bitch ass neighbor leaving too. He acted like he didn't even know who I was. And I called my mom, *Derrick*. She wasn't in car wreck. She's at home. Eating prunes. *Derrick*."

She stood over me fiercely. Then she rushed into the morgue only to come to an abrupt stop. She glared at the coroner's table, and there lay a lifeless, covered body.

"Who is that?" she blurted.

I crawled in, slowly getting to my feet as Canieya began to tear up.

"Who is that?" she repeated.

I traveled beside her, crying as I approached the table.

"Na, na…man. Who *is* that?" she groaned with a trembling voice.

I stood on the opposite side of the table to face her. I lifted the white sheet and folded it back to display the horrific scene. I looked down at Bookie's corpse without flinching as my tears diminished.

Canieya glared with skepticism for a moment. Then the crying began. She worked and struggled hard to conceal it. Her eyes started shuffling. She was devastated, and I could tell without even looking at her. She grabbed her mouth as she stumbled up to the table. She gagged as the tears rolled down her elegant face. She rubbed her hand through Bookie's hair.

She shook like crazy as her fingers tripped through the disfigured gashes.

I gripped the crown of Bookie's head, turning the wound toward Canieya. She dropped to her knees, bending over as if she had been fatally stabbed.

Just then, the two agents exited the morgue. But I stood still, gazing at her, almost completely separated from life. Finally, I turned Bookie's head straight. My eye started twitching, and my finger tapped against the edge of the coroner's table.

I was pissed.

Canieya screamed to the top of her lungs, rolling uncontrollably on the floor.

Now, Canieya crazy. I told y'all already. Something wrong with that bitch. She got bit by a rattler once. Never went to the hospital. Never died.

But in her defense, I may have caused some of this crazy. This was a pain that no mom should have to endure. In all, I guess it would be safe to say I kind of expected this reaction.

"WWwhhhyyyy! WHhhhYYYyy! God!! No!" she yelled in agony. Then the yelling stopped, and I was still out of the moment.

She stood to her feet only to see me…the loser, standing in complete grief. It was all my fault.

She spat in my face.

I didn't react.

"You did this. You!" she stated as she stopped crying. "Damn you, Crane!"

She stepped closer to me. And at this point, I couldn't look at her. But I stood steadfast and void of all emotion.

She jacked me up by the collar, shaking me like a rag doll.

She shouted obscenities to the highest of levels as I fell back into a stainless-steel chair.

I was so drained from crying and utterly mortified by the image of Bookie's corpse.

Canieya had been swinging on me the whole time I was gripping with my mistake.

She head-butted me in the face, breaking my nose.

She punched and slapped me to a bloody slush.

"Fuck! Crane! Damn YOU! Fuck you to hell, Crane! I hate

your guts! Fuck Crane! FUuuccckkk!" she screamed.

I sat lifeless, as if Canieya wasn't even there. All I could see was the killer's face as she delivered her destructive punching.

I couldn't feel anything.

"Fucking Crane! Destroying everything, everywhere you go! Damn, I **hate** you!" she bellowed.

She continued her attack as the agents barged into the morgue. "Whoa! Heyy!" Woods shouted as they rushed in.

They grabbed her by the arms and lifted her into the air.

Bish!

She kicked me dead in the jaw with those steel thigh-high boots.

Blood spewed from my mouth as she shouted, "Fuck you, Crane! Fuck You! Let me go! Let me go! Damn it! I'm gonna kill you, Crane! You're about to join her!"

She then grabbed Lockley by his coat collar and flipped him over her shoulder, slamming him into the wall.

"Aaaaggghhhh!" Lockley hollered as he sunk to the floor.

Agent Woods released Canieya, throwing his hands up as if he were under arrest.

Canieya whirled around, looking at me in a complete rage.

I just stared at Bookie with my bloody, bruised face.

Canieya was breathing heavily while Agent Woods backed away with his hands still up.

Lockley wallowed on the floor before clambering up to his feet. He stood slowly, slumping over with his hands on his knees. He posted up against the wall panting for air. And then everyone stared at me. I sat without a soul, branding this demonic day.

Canieya pulled out her hair. "Aaaaaggggghhhhhhh!" she screamed as the hair follicles plucked from her scalp and drifted to the floor. "What the fuck happened, Crane?"

"Crane?" Lockley interjected. "Wait. *Arlo* Crane?"

"Oh boy." Woods scowled as Lockley continued.

"This man is wanted in countless states. He's —"

"Shut the fuck up!" Canieya boomed as she snapped over to Lockley. "Crane's mine. You understand me! Don't fucking touch him!"

The agents glared with confusion.

"Agreed?" she screamed.

"Yes," Woods replied as Canieya turned back to me, huffing.

She walked up to me and sat in my lap, facing me with her hands on her hips. "Talk," she whispered, but I sat speechless.

"Talk, Crane…," she begged as the tears dropped from her face. She wiped them away roughly, as if she didn't want to cry.

Her overwhelming smell zapped me back to life, and only then did I indulge her with the informative bits of agonizing news. But as the moment passed, my explanation formed a connection.

"When I turned the corner, I saw a bright light."

"Like a window?" Canieya asked.

"Yeah… and it closed shut like some kinda —"

"Gateway." she added with fear. "I saw the same thing at LaGuardia. Guy walked clean out of it."

"It's Horace Vaydin. His assassins," Lockley whispered with a grunt. "They move with the shadows."

"That's the second time you said that shit." Canieya sniffed. "What do you mean, they move with the shadows?"

"Something about them. Their tech isn't normal," Woods noted.

"You mean, like, perverted?" Canieya asked as the morgue grew eerie.

"No," Woods disclosed. "They aren't from here…"

"When you say here, do you mean Earth?" Canieya said as the agents stood silent. "You mean to tell me we're dealing with aliens?"

"Just before Bookie died, I saw three of my friends vanish into thin air." I reported as I re-covered Bookie with the sheet. "Tom and I went back to the scene, and there was a faint neon color over the ground."

"Ha!" Canieya burst into laughter. "That's bullshit," she grumbled as the agents glared with worry.

Hesitantly I stuttered, "And… we saw the clouds…"

"What was wrong with the clouds?" Woods asked as he stood in an uncomfortable state.

"They were shaped like a massive doughnut. It looked like a hole in the sky."

"Evidently, something else is going on here," Canieya said as I stared on to my daughter's body. "And it ain't no damn aliens."

"Maybe we can help each other." I smirked as Canieya peered into me. "Like old times."

"This is not a drug sting," she replied. "You find who murdered our daughter. Leave Horace Vaydin to us."

"Those assassins are up to something grand," Lockley added. "And we're smack in the middle of it."

"What does he look like?" I asked as I reached into my coat pocket to retrieve the image.

"We don't know yet," Canieya stammered, humbling herself from my grisly expression.

I tucked the drawing back into my pocket as Canieya stepped closer to me and whispered, “I'm headed to a briefing now.”

And with a deep breath, she inhaled my mannish odor. And in turn, I took in her seductive essence. How could we resist each other with all that hot loving we used to make? Just the thought of us colliding in the science of romance would only…

Suddenly, the walls fell like a drawbridge over a moat.

We kissed fiercely and passionately, even with my bloody, disfigured face. It was as if we had never kissed before. Those deep sloppy tongues digging into each other's uvula.

“Euw,” Lockley screeched.

Canieya pushed me back and uttered, “You find him, Crane.” She caressed my chest, and fumbled over my abs. And just when she had grabbed me by my belt buckle, she reluctantly walked away.

This was her way of apologizing, and I knew I wasn't going to see her again. My eyes traveled up and down her breathtaking body as I captured my final glimpse of heaven and hell, perfectly integrated. Oh, you already know I grabbed her ass. It was so soft and fluffy. I knew she was mine 'cause she didn't even turn around to acknowledge me. Hell, it was almost like she expected it.

She stopped in front of the other agents and hissed, "Not a word…"

The agents nodded as she left the room. Then they scowled in shock as they finally came to grips with who I *really* was.

The blood fell in clumps from my face, tainting the white sheet that covered my daughter.

Agent Woods, shook his head in sorrow. "I'm sorry for your loss." He sighed with grief. Then he and Agent Lockley exited the morgue.

The door hydraulics and the air conditioning unit filled my ears. Right before the door fully shut, Canieya held it open. She stood for a moment, staring as I glanced up to make eye contact. The confirmation was definitive as she glared into my pulverized face of gloom. My eyes screamed over the silence as Canieya's lips began to tremble. She released the door and walked away in tears.

CHAPTER: 13

Fine!

You know, I've been scarred so much that crying really irks me. But that visit to Montefiore Medical was probably the saddest moment of my life.

From the backseat of Agent Woods' vehicle, I cried as we traveled through New York. Nothing had changed since I moved… Well, the poor had become more impoverished and the middle class seemed to be doing all the work. But the wealthy floated around in their little hover cars. Now this was the only upgrade that I didn't think I'd live to see. But the early integration was still in its testing phase.

The way they intermingled with the other cars was a straight-up nightmare. They had their own sensors, speed limit, and fuel pumps. But I could only smile at the advancements in technology. Those hover cars were meant for the wealthy. All I wanted was justice for my daughter, and to kill Horace Vaydin. With the way things were looking, I'd be doing the world a favor by cleansing it of his filth.

New York, NY: Lotte Palace

Agent Woods pulled into the valet parking. He popped the trunk of the car as he got out, shutting the door behind him. He grabbed all the bags from the trunk while Lockley carried a single briefcase. But surprisingly, he opened the door for me.

Agent Woods walked over and gave me a key. "Twenty-third floor," he announced as he proceeded through the sliding doors. I trailed in beside him as the valet patron drove off.

We entered the main lobby, which was quite unique in nature.

So much for secrecy.

We approached the elevator, and just as the doors opened, Agents Woods stepped in.

Lockley and I stood outside of the elevator, staring each other down. The doors began to close when Woods stuck his arm out to hold them open.

With purpose I continued my frightening gaze of a hellcat.

"After you," he said most politely.

Lockley followed behind as I stepped into the elevator.

The doors closed slowly as the calming; melodious music charged our ears. My body and soul fled into the ceiling as I tuned into this sound. Free from the accursed crime waves that relentlessly plagued our nation.

Agent Lockley opened his briefcase and passed me several photos. "These are satellite images of the most recent bombings. If you notice, they all appear to be similar in level of destruction."

"Yeah. The blast radius looks controlled," I muttered while passing the photos back.

The innocent elevator music flourished, tapping gracefully against our eardrums. Right then, a phone jingled. "Ah!" Woods chimed. "Ain't this some shit. That guy. The one you didn't kill."

"The one who asked for Crane?"

"Uh-huh. He just ratted. You heard of a guy named Matony?"

"Vince… 'Iceberg' Matony. Head of the Italian mob. We took out his drug supply on Primosa Street a while back."

"Well, that explains that," Woods grumbled.

"But how they get their hands on that tech?" I wondered.

"They may be in cahoots with Horace," Lockley replied as he placed the images into his briefcase. He then took out another photo.

"Matony's tying up loose ends. Good thing we got to you first," Woods boasted as Lockley handed me the other image.

"That's the figure," I confirmed. "This what I saw on my roof."

"We believe there's more of them," Lockley declared.

"You mean, more than one?" I quizzed while peering into the blurry picture.

"Yes. We caught him stepping out of one of those windows of light you described," Lockley answered as he placed the photo back into his briefcase.

"Then he vanished into the shadows." Woods added with a grim tone.

Ding!

The elevator doors opened. As we entered the hall, there were several agents standing in all black. They all wore the same poker face.

"We believe Vaydin has a record or a list of targets. He's making the task look effortless with the aid of these assassin," Woods confessed.

"He wants to a-sass-a nation," Lockley quipped.

"So… am I on this list?" I asked.

"Maybe, maybe not. It's more likely someone you're close to, or maybe someone you know," Lockley noted.

"Crane," I replied.

"This group is advanced. I wouldn't doubt that they

already know we're here," Lockley stressed. "That's why we got security on your floor and the one below."

As much as I hated to hear his voice of vomitus gargle, I honestly had to admit he was right. But the thought of taking out these so-called assassins had me smiling with delight.

Just as we reached my room, I glanced to my key. We came to a stop as I inserted the card into the door panel.

As I gently opened the door, Agent Woods announced, "Madam, your staying quarters."

From the outside, this room was way smaller than I had anticipated. But the suite expanded with glorious detail.

My jaw dropped, and my eyes stretched to take in the full sight.

We stepped in, and I flipped the light switch on the wall.

The room was marvelous. I gasped gently, panning across the setting.

"Nice," I whispered.

The room had a separate kitchen, a long hallway, a dining room, a living room, and a gorgeous balcony that revealed an even more alluring view of the city. This was the whole nine yards. Marble floors, priceless furniture with gold trimmings, and massive paintings on the walls.

Woods sat the hefty duffel bag on the coffee table next to a bowl of fruit. Then he sat the other duffel bag on the dining room table. He unzipped the bag on the coffee table and set up a laptop on a nearby computer desk.

Lockley sighed, flopping ferally into the chair at the living room table. He unzipped the other bag and unloaded a throng of weapons onto the table.

Lockley glared at Woods. "Are we not gonna talk about this?" he mumbled as he propped the butt of a rifle on his knee.

"Talk about what?" replied Woods.

Right then, I took a green apple from the bowl of fruit on the coffee table. While heading down the hallway, I bit into the apple.

"Crane…," whispered Lockley.

"Look, man, she's having a rough day. I'm sure this can wait." Woods pulled an odd device from the duffel bag. It sort of looked like a thumb drive. "What's this?" he wondered aloud. He shrugged and placed the drive on the coffee table next to the fruit bowl.

Lockley continued to stare at Woods. I could sense the texture of his covetous hands, fumbling through my essence.

While approaching the hall closet, I opened the door and bit into the apple again. Then I overheard the agents whispering.

"He is a wanted man. And if we don't turn him in, we could become accessories."

Confidently, I entered the living room and propped myself against the wall.

"You guys thinking 'bout turning me in?" I quizzed as I took another bite. With my arms folded, I waited for them to answer.

"I'm not in on this," Woods yelled from the dining room.

"We don't want to be an accomplice to said crimes," Lockley jeered. "And if we turn him in, that means… Hey, wait a minute. You're the reason why Crane was never arrested!"

Gripping the apple with my teeth, I bit deep into the fruit. Then I gawked to the floor. "Yeah."

"You've been covering for him," Lockley continued as I chewed away. "Haven't you?!"

The room went silent, all except for my eating.

"Woods knew," I pointed out. "Your superiors, too."

"What?" Lockley shouted.

"It's true," Woods mumbled. "Chief Goodrum told me."

"You knew? And didn't tell me?"

"I vowed to keep it secret."

"If you turn in Crane, you might as well turn me in, too," I said. "Hell! Turn in Woods and Chief Goodrum while ya' at it."

"Chris Lockley," Woods mumbled under his breath. "You

remember when that money came up missing from the evidence room?"

"Yeah."

"And you were short on your mortgage?"

"What does that have to do with anything?" Lockley bellowed.

"That was me. I took the money to pay for your mortgage…"

"Wow!" I shouted as I bit into the apple.

"Why'd you take that money?" cried Lockley.

Woods shrugged. "Saw a friend in need. But Crane is more valuable outside of prison. He's a necessary evil."

"This can't be happening," Lockley fretted.

"We have the pleasure of working with one of the most esteemed agents in the field," Woods chatted. "She was just attacked in the airport, and she just lost her only child. Don't be so insensitive. Be a friend… See my need."

My eyes teared up as Lockley sat the gun in his lap. He shook his head and took a deep breath.

"Are these my shoes? In the hall closet?" I hummed and sniffed with a mouthful of apple.

"Yeah!" Woods shouted. "We figured we would have to change your wardrobe, seeing that you do have a change of identity." He then reached into his pocket. "Almost forgot." He walked over to me and passed me another set of keys.

"Did you really steal that money," I whispered.

"You mean from the evidence room? Na…" Woods replied softly. "Your new car is parked on deck B." He smiled as the keys dangled in front of my eyes.

"Is it red?" I shouted while chomping into the apple.

He nodded. "Yep."

"Does it matter?" Lockley hollered from the living room.

Standing abruptly, I snatched the keys from Agent Woods and roared, "Excuse me!"

Woods gestured in an *'after you'* fashion as I trampled over to Lockley.

"What's with yo' bitch ass?"

Lockley stood to his feet, still holding that assault rifle.

"I wish a muthafucka' would!" I hollered, stepping in front of him. "I know you don't like me. You think I'm dirty for harboring Crane."

"That's not it," he replied.

Agent Woods walked in as my neck got involved with my denigrating speech. "I didn't know I was gonna have to deal with this shit!" I pointed like I was about to chop something. Then, with a booming howl, I shouted, "Damn, I should've stayed in London!"

"No," Woods cried as he leaned against the wall.

I threw my hands up in despair, tossing my keys to the floor. The juice from my apple slapdash on my arm. "Why I gotta fool with his stupid ass?"

Lockley wiped his mouth as Woods shook his head, putting his hands in his pockets.

"You either accept this situation, or I walk!" I continued.

"Okay, I understand," Lockley said in dismay.

"Oh, I don't think you do," I shouted, standing dead in his face. "My daughter is dead! I was attacked by a group of hoodlums while your ass was off eating milk and cookies. You wanna catch Horace Vaydin? Then pull your shit together!!"

"Fine," Lockley replied.

"Fine!!!" I loudly repeated, fiercely biting my apple.

Then I hurried to the kitchen because I saw myself stuffing the rest of my apple up his ass and leaving it there for him to shit out. Agent Woods followed behind me, rubbing his hand through his hair.

The apple zapped past him.

Bok!

"Whoa!" he shouted as it burst against the wall. "Agent Lawson, you should get some rest. Let's pick up tomorrow," Woods said as I opened the refrigerator. "How's eight o'clock?"

"Make it nine," I grumbled while slamming shit around in the fridge.

CHAPTER: 14

Disclosure

The Bronx, New York:
Crane's Residence

A silk red ribbon, tied about a bottle of wine, sat in the center of my kitchen table.

"Vera and I wanted you to have this," Tom whimpered as he sat at the opposite end of the table. "We don't want you to drink your life away…We just wanted you to know that we care."

"Thanks, Tom," I said softly as my eyes started to water.

"Have you heard anything from the authorities? I know it's been about sixty years now," he joked with a smirk. "Surely they've made some type of connection."

"Just the drawn image… That's about it."

"Damn. Hey, can I get some water?"

"All I got is tap," I answered as I stood slowly.

"I know this has got to be a lot, Derrick. I have a child, too. I couldn't imagine losing Tela. I can't figure out why something like this could happen to you. You didn't do anything," he expressed as I approached the sink. "If you need anything, you let me know. I mean it, man. My family and I are here for you."

Poor Tom. He was still calling me Derrick. I felt the urge to tell him the truth. Yet, the truth was maintained by my indisputable conditions.

Tom's eyes and his solid unyielding face convicted me as I

took a glass from the dish rack. Tom shook his head as I turned on the water. It ran lively from the faucet, but I stood there, peeking out the window and into the sky.

I closed the blinds and stared lifelessly at the wall, then over to my cell phone, still plugged into the charger. My mind was jumbled with uncoupled thoughts. How could they just disappear like that?

"How's that water coming?"

"Ah! My bad." I yelped as I stuck the glass under the faucet.

"What we saw was a bit… Unearthly." Tom chuckled as I sat the glass of water on the table.

He slid the glass over as I stood in front of the sink.

Tom took a sip of his water and sat back in the old rickety chair, as his leg jumped nervously. "Oh! Vera had Okani's car towed back to the house. Forgot to tell you."

"That's cool." I mumbled. After turning off the water, I dried my hands. Then I grabbed a chair and sat at the opposite end of the table.

"Turns out, Vera and Okani went to the same school."

"Didn't know that." I spoke. "Her keys are over there. On

the counter."

"Okay… Have you called Canieya? To set up any funeral arrangements?"

Then I almost stopped breathing.

"What's wrong? Aw man… that was too soon," Tom mumbled. He just sat there, breathing with agitation, as I dwelled on my venomous thinking.

"Uh, I didn't mean to say that," he whispered.

"My name isn't Derrick." I retorted with anger.

Tom looked awfully confused as I regained my focus. "Who are you, then?"

"Don't act like you don't know," I bluntly stated. "I'm a wanted man. A fugitive. I've committed many crimes, and I have assisted in numerous criminal activities. The police are looking for me and I would rather they shoot me on sight."

Tom began to crumble as I looked vividly through his soul.

"I'm a dangerous and unstable recovering crackhead. My life is ruined. My daughter is dead because of me and my numerous enemies. You, Tom, are probably the only friend I have. And I don't want to endanger you or your family. I must… I must ask you to leave. There's no help for me."

Tom kept sitting there as if he was in denial, like he didn't hear me. He was looking down to the table, holding on to his glass of water.

A rip of duct tape trashed his ears as I snatched my 9mm from under the table.

Wham!

I slammed the gun on the table, sloshing water from his glass. "Tom!" I hollered, startling his head up. "Please leave."

He looked at the gun and then at me with a face of fear. A terror like none other beat his eyes open.

"Please…," I begged.

He began to tear up, and so did I.

Tom was truly a good person. He was a good friend that was only concerned about my well-being. This was why I had to free him from my hellraising. My lies. My contaminated task of purification. And my demonic, God-challenging excuse of a life.

Tom sat persistently in grief. He dropped his head slowly as a tear dampened the table. I felt myself growing all emotional. My undesirable truths disgraced Tom. But before I could come to tears, I exploded.

"Now!" I screamed while snatching up the gun and cocking it in one motion.

He pushed back from the table. Throwing his hands up, he

stood slowly. "Okay! Okay…" he bellowed. "Well… I guess that's it," he whispered as he backed up to the kitchen counter. With his eyes on me, he grabbed Okani's keys. "I'll just… give these to Vera."

He tucked the keys in his pocket as I stood in the kitchen, holding the gun so tight that my hand shook. Tom knew then that I was something else. A loner. A neglected crackhead, rebounding in youth but full of remorse and uncharted anger.

We continued to stare into each other's eyes.

Tom forlornly grabbed the doorknob as he gawked to the floor. Then, still procrastinating, he opened the door and turned into the nightlight. He cracked open the rickety screen door with a face of dejection. "We ain't friends no more?"

With a guttural tone I yelled, "Fuck you sayin', bruh?"

Tom stepped softly out of my house, closing the screen door behind him. But I couldn't discern anything. All I could see was red.

"You take care of yourself, Derrick, or whatever your name is," he said as he walked over to his house.

Friendless, I stood there, alone and out of tears. Then I placed the gun on the kitchen table and I looked around at my filthy house.

The walls were filled with holes where I had taken out my frustration on the sheetrock. My hand started to shake as I gawked at the bottle of wine sitting on the kitchen table.

Suddenly, reality struck a hard chord.

And I lost it.

I yanked up the bottle of wine and flung it into the wall.

Skkkaaashh!

Then I ripped the refrigerator out of the wall and picked it up over my head.

Boom!

The refrigerator dented the floor as I tossed it into the living room. The little food I had, strayed abroad. Then I yanked the microwave out the wall and tossed it directly through the window.

Bissssh!

Into the living room I ran, kicking over the couch. I snatched the flat screen TV from the wall. The cord whipped through the air as I shattered the screen with my head.

The gashes in my forehead bled as I tossed the TV into the kitchen. It crashed into pieces, bouncing off the oven and then to the ground.

"Derrick!" Tom screamed as he re-entered through the screen door.

He tackled me to the floor as I launched the coffee table across the room.

Ka-Dddiiiisssshcccc!!!

It crashed into the wall, shattering the nearby mirror.

He held me tight around the arms in his attempt to settle the mindless beast within me.

My tear ducts ran dry as we squabbled violently over the disgusting glass-covered floor. The smell of expensive wine and lint filled my nostrils. My forehead bled, staining the carpet as we rolled about.

"It's okay, champ… it's okay," Tom whispered as he hugged me to a tranquil still.

He huffed in my ear as I emotionally dismantled. "I gotcha, homie. I gotcha…"

CHAPTER: 15

The Hit List

New York, NY: Lotte Palace
Canieya's Suite

A few hours later, I sat in a sudsy bubble bath. Just me and my rage, cursing out loud.

My nerves were shot. Because I really wanted to relax but my curiosity for the gear left me spellbound. My aesthetic sense had yet to finish marveling.

After my bath, I dried myself off while approaching the walk-in closet within the master bedroom.

"This is almost too much," I said, glancing through the hundreds of dresses and blouses.

Then I kneeled to notice another array of shoes. "Oh, stilettos—my favorite. Someone really knows me." I chuckled.

Finally, I slipped into a silky white nightgown and tied up my hair before venturing back into the master bedroom.

While picking up the TV remote, I noticed there wasn't a TV. After pressing the power button, a large rectangle jutted from the wall. Camouflaged in form, the large panel flipped over, revealing a TV on the opposite side.

The TV came on as I dropped the remote, again engulfed in splendor.

Was it suspended in midair?

It pivoted and turned with me as I walked cautiously up to

the TV.

"Nice," I said, waving my hand between the open space of the wall and the TV. Then I wiped my hand under and above the TV. Even so, no brackets or mounts… Just nothing.

Bemused beyond reasoning, I stepped back from the TV mumbling, "What the hell…"

A ghostly feeling toyed with my soul, fluttering like paper in the wind.

There truly was no explanation for this beauty favoring my resting area.

Magnets maybe…

After staring at the TV, I walked into the living room.

Standing over the coffee table, I gazed into the duffel bag of weapons. And from what I could tell, they had never been fired.

I loaded a few of them, testing the aim and weight. Then I put the larger guns back into the duffel bag and I sat it on the floor beside the living room couch. That's when I noticed the device sitting by the fruit bowl on the coffee table.

As I walked over to the computer desk, I took the device from the coffee table. Then, without taking my eyes off the device, I reached back for the rolling chair. Turning the chair toward me, I took a seat, and scooted up to the computer desk.

As the computer booted up, I looked at the device again and buttoned it into the small pocket of my nightgown.

I grabbed a bottle of Bottega Gold Prosecco from the cooler next to the computer desk. I stripped off the tab and removed the cage. Then I retrieved a rock glass from the kitchen cupboard. Glancing over to the computer, I rinsed out the glass and sat it next to the sink.

Then I took a towel from the kitchen drawer to remove the prosecco's cork. I draped the towel over the bottle and held the cork in place. While twisting the base of the bottle, a portion of the cork crumbled away. I tossed the towel on the counter and sat the bottle next to the rock glass.

"Where are you?" I pondered.

Foraging for a corkscrew, I looked on the computer desk, about the living room, and in the kitchen.

Suddenly, the computer sounded.

My search ended as I rushed back over to the computer.

And there it was, sitting on the computer desk. The corkscrew... I picked it up while loading the odd device into the computer tower. The computer immediately recognized the drive.

Then, a cool breeze washed through the room as I glanced over to the balcony door.

The curtains flapped about in the windy gust as I trekked

over slowly. "Wasn't this closed?"

As I slid the door shut, the computer sounded.

Locking the door, I sprinted over to the computer, setting the corkscrew back on the desk.

Tons of files had been copied onto the device. There was shit all over the place. Folders and folders of stuff and documents that I don't think I was supposed to see. There were diagrams of spaceships, bikes, vessels, and computers made of light. I even saw a PDF document containing images of the floating TV that I just saw in the master bedroom.

What the hell was this?

Within an instant, I was glued to this display of futuristic data, which had now become a discreet pile of blitzing information. My recent findings truncated the room's opulence to almost nothing.

But I searched through the device with an unyielding effort. The more I uncovered, the more I rummaged.

"Transportal Device… Universal remotes. TPD(s). Communicates with radio waves to exact a definite point in space. The fuck? Converting radio waves into light? Light into tachyons, and then tachyons into portals with gateway properties?" I mumbled as I searched through the folders.

"The Symbassy? Complete autocracy over all walks of life, amalgaming every reality via a governing body. Powerful spies with unlimited reach… Political control spans across countless galaxies. Project Rapture? A Xaris plot designed to cease control over a planet. Symbassy quest for universal tyranny???" I gasped with suspense. "Triple Beam blueprints. Revamped designs for holocaustic purposes? What the hell?"

My words were replaced with vigorous breathing.

Now the information on this device had reached a level beyond that of extreme classification. This was so bad that I started to question ever accessing the drive. This sadistic treasure chest brought a startling feeling of discomfort. But then my vexation soared as I stumbled upon a folder. It was abnormally colored black and with a fiendish label suspiciously titled—

"The Hit List?" I mumbled.

For seconds I hesitated. Then, out of curiosity, I double-clicked the folder.

A window popped up, asking for a password.

With discontent, I sat back in the rolling chair.

But I was afraid to start typing into the entry field, because I could lose the entire file due to some form of encryption.

Full of frustrated wind, I propped up my elbows on the edge of the desk, catching my head in my hands. Staring down at the keyboard, I breathed roughly.

I'm no hacker. Shit, I hadn't been trained for that yet. And trampling over myself with mindless failure was not about to generate a password.

But I wanted in on this file.

Sitting up from my depressing state, I tried to pierce the computer screen with my convicting eyes. My glare lasted for so long the computer almost went to sleep.

What should I do? The first thing I could think of… I clicked the ENTER key.

The folder popped open.

My heart dropped into my stomach. The folder had no password at all. I engaged the computer again, scooting the rolling chair deeper into the desk. I couldn't get any closer.

There were names of people I had put away. Each name was accompanied by a folder that contained some very confidential and sensitive information. Every name was in alphabetical order: the last name first, first name last. There were people from all over the world on this list. Even some of my old supervisors.

After hours of searching, I started to doze off. Then I

reached the *C* section. My tired eyes washed anew, as if I was about to see something horrific. And there it was…

"Crane...," I whispered.

Right then I grabbed my cell phone from my purse and dialed.

"Pick up the phone." I huffed, pacing the floor just as the phone went to voicemail.

"Crane! They're coming for you. Horace Vaydin, Matony, and some kinda Za-karachas or some shit. The windows of light. They got some kind of a Project Rapture. Talking about taking over the Earth with a Triple Beam or something. They gotta Hit List. Crane… you're on the list. You need to get outta —" The voicemail timed out. "Shit!"

Tossing my phone on the computer desk, I sat abruptly into the seat. This titanic freakshow of horrifying data had overwhelmed me to the point of wanting to stop, but I just had to know.

For a while I scrolled until I grew weary. Then I typed my name into the search engine…

Last name first and then first name last.

The computer parsed, loaded, and stabilized its systematic review. The device became so unreal, so immorally sinful, and vile that I dared to admit to my findings. But my name was there. My stomach dropped into my pelvis. Quickly I stood, rolling the chair back to a clumsy blunder.

My breathing got panicky because I couldn't open the folder with my name.

"No!!" I cried as I felt myself vomiting.

My night had become something else as I snatched the device from the computer in anger.

Suddenly, a figure dashed across the balcony.

Stumbling back into the rolling chair, I focused as hard as I could on the area outside the window. It could've just been the curtains swaying.

Nawl… I ain't crazy.

Tiptoeing over to the sliding door, I tucked the device into my nightgown pocket.

"Agent Woods? Lockley? This better not be some stupid-ass joke!" I yelled, peeking down the hall to the master bedroom and then back to the balcony door.

My heart pounded out of my chest as I clenched on to the drive. Did I even see anything?

Hoping to gain some sort of clarity, I replayed the image of the figure in my head. Something dashed by the window, but I just couldn't tell what it was.

"Hey!!" I repeated, sticking my head out into the palace hallway. All the agents had left for the night.

Suddenly, the lady across the hall cracked her door open and stuck her head out into the hallway.

I charged over to her, screaming, "What the fuck, bitch!!"

She shut the door fast, locking it with tremendous speed.

Turning abruptly, I stomped back into my room. As I shut the door and locked it, the thought to relay the occurrence crossed my mind. That's when I snatched up my cell phone from the desk. But I was too proud and stubborn to call any of my colleagues.

"I'm spooked, all right?!" I shouted.

Darting into the kitchen, I sat my cell phone on the counter. I grabbed a saber knife from the magnet rack above the sink and seared open the bottle of Prosecco.

Possssh!

The sound of the cork popping reconstituted my mind as I placed the saber knife on the kitchen table. Then I grabbed the rock glass from the sink. While strolling over to the computer, my hands trembled as I filled the glass, spilling wine everywhere.

I sat the glass of bubbly on the desk and drank from the bottle instead.

Gulping fiercely, I eyed the balcony. Then I lowered the bottle and paused to study the corkscrew.

Walking over to the adjacent couch, I sat there to monitor

the window again. Propping the bottle upon my knee, I periodically took an aggressive gulp. It was like I was drinking water.

I took out the device and stared at it again, then the balcony door, then the computer, and then the corkscrew. The computer was innocent; I wanted to hate it, but I couldn't. I felt violated and disrespected. Motionlessly I gazed at the computer screen until it dimmed into hibernation.

With a smirk, I shook my head in denial. "Aliens…that's crazy."

Was I tripping? Maybe I was seeing shit.

Tucking the device back into my nightgown pocket, I buttoned it closed, then I gulped more of the Prosecco. It tickled on the way down as the cold liquid spilled about the corners of my nervous lips.

All I had to do was go to sleep. Nine o'clock would be here before you know it.

While facing the balcony, I sat for another moment. The thought of my bedroom jogged through my head, as I cautiously arose from the couch.

Stumbling to the suite's door, I assured myself that it was

locked. After grabbing my cell phone from the kitchen counter, I bumbled and teetered through the hall, and straight to the master bedroom. Those zesty sheets of solace were my only true friends.

After setting the alarm clock, I placed my phone on the nightstand. Then, with the bottle of Prosecco in hand, I clambered into the cold sheets to remedy my zonked body. Lying on my side, hoping to forget all this foolishness, I continued my vigil, peering into the doorway. From the cozy confines of my bedding, I watched for the slightest movement.

Recalling my visit to the hospital, I began to tear up again. But my anger wiped my tears dry as I gripped the device in my pocket like I wanted to break it. My grip grew even tighter just to keep my tears from resurfacing.

As my anger receded, the windows to my soul grew heavy. My body heat brought the silken fabrics to a toasty chill. I dropped the bottle of Prosecco to the smooth carpet. It barely sounded as it rolled under the bed. The fight to maintain my hawk-eyed devotion was lost. My eyes closed without notice, and my dreams began, slowly but surely.

CHAPTER: 16

Wraith
Part 1

The Bronx, New York:
Crane's Residence- 8:00 a.m.

Several thumbtacks fixed the hand-drawn image of my daughter's killer to the wall. The image and I stared at each other through the night. At 8:30 in the morning, I caught myself sitting on the living room floor, still glaring at the image.

Tom had left me alone to wallow in my own filth. With all this crazy shit happening, I didn't blame him. My friends had vanished into thin air. Thin. Air! Maybe it was magic, or…

My daughter was dead and needed to be buried. Canieya was back in town and possibly on to something. Speaking of Canieya… I took my gaze off the image, jumped up from the floor, and darted into the kitchen.

Snatching my cell from the charger, I powered it on. My eyes grew with intensity as I listened to Canieya's voicemail.

"Triple Beam?" I grumbled while returning her call.

Lotte Palace
Canieya's Suite

RRriiiiinnnnnggg!!!!!

RRriiiiinnnnnggg!!!!!

Awaken by Crane's ringtone, my eyes stretched wide and-

"AAAAgggggghhhhh!" I screamed as a figure hurtled from the ceiling.

Fwooommm!

The sheets entangled my legs as I tripped to the floor.

The bed weighed down as if an asteroid had landed.

There was a demonic katana piercing through the mattress, snaring a significant chunk of my hair.

My eyes locked on to a ninja, with a stifling mist lifting from his baking figure. He wore an all-black, formfitting ninja *yoroi*, with black razor-incrusted shin guards, and matching vambraces shielding his scary hands. He was large and lanky, with a black utility belt clipped about his waist and a sinister mask covering his face. His pixelated sun-red eyes squinted with a perplexing glow.

My phone continued to ring as the assailant turned to glare

in my face. The sight of this frightening assassin scared me stiff. But a massive bucket of adrenaline took a shit in my backyard.

I leapt to my feet, snatching the sheets with me.

His sword raked through the fabric like a slicing machine.

Falling to my back, I immediately thrusted myself up.

I spun around.

Vmf!

The fiend popped up in front of me.

He swiped for my head as I slid through his legs.

He followed, with a downward thrust snagging a piece of my nightgown.

Struggling to my feet, I took off into the hall.

He caved into the walls, blasting up turmoil behind me. Swiping wickedly with that demonic blade, he destroyed ceramics, and pictures with ease.

He ran even faster with his evil powerful legs, vaulting from wall to wall.

Entering the living room, he landed on the couch in front of me, jump kicking into the air.

With my wrist across my chest, I blocked as he fractured my forearm, forcing me back into the hall.

Charging back in, I engaged this high-paced fray.

He swung his sword to chop off my head.

But I ducked with a punch to the gut. "Ya!"

My hand reduced to mush. But the pain faded fast as we danced violently across the floor.

My bones cracked and shattered with every strike I made.

Catching my fist in mid-swing, he tossed me, kata-guruma style, over his shoulder.

Ka-Bang!

I leveled the coffee table, jolting the room. As my phone rang, he thrust his sword.

"YA!" he shouted, piercing through the floor as I rolled to recovery.

The demon punched me in the stomach, zapping me across the room.

Croom!

Crushing into the sheetrock with force, I dismantled the wall behind me. Easing into the room next door, I latched on to the remaining wall and plunged myself, back into this deadly brawl.

Crane's Residence

"Pick up the phone…"

'Dis' Canieya. I ain't answering. Bye! – The person you are calling does not answer. Please leave a message after the tone."

Beep!!

"Candy, the hell you talking 'bout? I gotta triple beam in the kitchen. We use that shit to weigh dope. Yo! Just call me back when you get this… All right? Peace."

My feelings took me by surprise as I hung the phone up. The sad part was that I was so excited to call her that I didn't think about what she had said.

After sitting the phone on the counter, I came to a stop… My eyes fixed on to the image tacked to the wall in the living room. My lips trembled with anger as I dropped my head. And before I knew it, my eyes teared up…

Reaching slowly for the phone, I zoned into the image again. Then I froze stiff.

Lotte Palace
Canieya's Suite

The ninja stabbed for my gut. As I sidestepped, he punctured the wall.

Snatching the clamp from my hair, I slashed through his neck as he plucked his sword free. He yanked me up by the neck and flung me like a shoebox.

I flipped through the air, while reaching for the front door.

Crash!

The bookshelf exploded as I crushed through the wall. Bouncing off the kitchen floor, I slid to a halt. Blood spewed from my mouth, covering the tiles as I gasped for air. Then I sat up, still reaching for the doorknob. But I was clearly facing the wrong way.

It felt like I had been run over by a Zamboni machine. He must've punctured my lungs.

Just then, my vigor returned with a zest. I pinned my hair up with the hair clamp. Then I stood quickly, yanking two cast-iron skillets from the pot rack above the kitchen island.

My phone rang faintly as I turned to face the kitchen entrance…

Crane's Residence

The cabinet swung open as I lifted the triple beam from the shelf. With my phone up to my ear, I sat the device on the counter. Just as I studied over the contraption, Canieya's voicemail began.

"Dis' Canieya. I ***said*** *I aint answering. Bye!"*

Beep!!

"Sorry to keep calling you. That last message was a little sporadic," I said, attempting to keep my cool. "And how you get your voicemail to change? Yo, can we look over that hit list? Maybe we can track down Matony and some of those cats and put a stop this shit. And we need to get Bookie's funeral arranged, too. I know you're upset. She was my responsibility… Trust me, no one's hurting worse than ya' boy. I just wish you'd answer…I need —"

The voicemail timed out as I sat the phone on the counter next to the triple beam. After turning to face the living room, it hit me. Bookie's killer was sent for me.

While lost in the image stapled to the living room wall, I picked up my cell again and walked over to the drawing.

The bones wiggled in my hands as I gripped the skillets by the handles. With my eyes glued to the kitchen entrance, I spat blood to the floor while tiptoeing ahead.

Vmff!

The assassin emerged out of nowhere.

I stumbled back as he studied me from the kitchen entrance. It was then when I thought that he could be inhuman. Popping up out of nowhere isn't just unfeasible, but it denounces all Earthly principles. But I was determined to win. He fucked up my morning.

"C'mon!" I shouted.

He shot over, instantly engaging in combat.

The skillets slowed me as I blocked his demonic attacks. I roundhouse-kicked him in the face, fracturing my heel.

I whacked him in the face with the cookware, the vibration shook my grip loose.

It stunned him as I struck again with the other skillet.

He blocked and swung his blade toward my throat.

Staggering back into the sink, I reached to turn on the

water.

He slashed into my forearm.

"Ahhhhh!!!" I screamed, snatching my hand back.

He kicked me into the refrigerator.

My ribs snapped as I whirled around, grabbing the fridge handle. As I opened the door, he charged into the fridge's frame, pinning me in the corner.

I reached over the door and whacked him repeatedly across the head with the skillet.

He sliced the skillet in half like a fire searing butter.

Discarding the broken skillet, I reached overhead and swung the freezer door open. It struck him in the face and closed.

I front-kicked the refrigerator door into him. He sliced with his sword, splitting the door in two, filleting away a portion of my thigh.

He kicked me into the oven, cracking my sternum.

The refrigerator door fell, scattering food everywhere. He stabbed into the oven behind me when I sidestepped.

Jerking the oven door open, I busted his blade while snatching out the oven rack.

Thwack!

I pulverized his face as the blow vibrated the rack from my hand.

He yanked his broken blade from the oven as I sprinted

by, reaching for the front door.

He grabbed me by my nightgown, and I slid to a stop.

My feet passed over my head as he launched me back into the oven.

"NNNooooo!!!"

Blaf!

I slid down the oven door as it slammed shut.

Somehow, I stood to my feet as he mended his sword to anew.

He attacked me from close quarters. I ducked and dodged for my life.

He stabbed for the kill, thrusting his sword for my stomach. I clapped my hands around his blade, counterbalancing the strength of his push.

Lifting parallel with his sword, I aligned myself with exquisite balance.

The frictional heat from the sword scorched through my palms as I cartwheeled over his shoulder.

I ducked into a tumble as he swung over my head, cutting into the countertop.

Rolling to the edge of the kitchen island, I stood and

snatched the saber knife from the counter.

We turned in unison as I pitched the knife through the air.

"Hah!"

Stazz!

The knife bashed into his face, pinning him to the side of the refrigerator.

As I whirled around, there stood a woman, slashing for my head.

"SHiittt!!" I hollered, slipping to my back.

Cluggg!

A blade lanced into the cupboard beside me.

Vmff!

She vanished, yanking her blade from the cabinet.

Immediately, I scrambled to my feet. My blood drained to the floor, as the first assassin wrenched the knife from his face. He chunked it to the floor as the second assassin popped up in the kitchen entrance.

She was gorgeous.

She stood about five-six. Her lips and facial structures were perfectly aligned. Her eyes were unnaturally large, brown and red with a twirling, twinkling varnish of failed blinking. Her hair was like a bright sun, shaped into two large afro puffs. She was a stallion, built like an Amazonian machine of war.

Her clothing was strange and not of Earthly fashion at all. She wore a cropped jacket, stitched with a bizarre brown fabric. The garment was full of razor-sharp zippers. And the sleeves were rolled up to her forearms. She wore a feathery white shirt underneath, with a chunky beige utility belt clamped around her waist. She wore a pair of off-white jika-tabi boots that were somehow fused into her pants. There was obviously something wrong with her expression, her overall texture. Her skin… It looked crystallized. And her eyes were… pixelated.

She flipped out a set of nunchakus and began a dangerous introduction of martial artistry. After her beautiful establishment, she held the nunchakus in front of her, and a pair of blades sprung from the ends.

But I was so distracted by a hissing noise that I failed to notice the two assassins approaching. Their enchanted hidden speed was like moving without moving.

But then, they froze and stared at me as the hissing continued.

Sssssssssss…

"Great," I blurted while glancing to the door, hoping to escape.

I stood boldly between my attackers. Wiping the blood from my mouth, I blew the rest of my hair out of my face.

Popping my neck, I grew cocky, taunting my aggressors.

"Come get me," I stated.

The meticulous attack grew hypnotizing.

Ssssssssssss…

Then it came!

They swiped lethally as I dodged the male assassin, but that bitch was too fast! She sliced across my forehead as the first assassin roundhouse-kicked me in the face.

The second assassin swung her nunchaku as I rolled around her and into the living room. I bolted to the door, but the first assassin German suplexed me back into the kitchen.

Whom!

The tiles cracked as I rolled overhead and to my feet. Jetting for the door, the second assassin jump-kicked me in the chest as I blocked with my injured body.

She sliced for my head. I duck and spun right into the first assassin's slash.

He cut my chest open, backing me into the sink.

Then he stabbed at me with his sword as I spun with a dodge. But the second assassin came fast, flailing those bladed nunchakus.

"Fuck!!" I screamed, ducking and dodging.

I spun around her, landing my back against the wall next to the kitchen entrance.

She sliced the wall into shreds. Then she diced across my belly.

"AAgghh!!!"

She cut me across the face so bad that I began to faint.

In my weakness, I fell to the floor, as the first assassin stabbed for my head. He thrusted into the wall as I stumbled to the door. I was inches away from the door knob when a strange commotion rumbled behind me. It sounded like a factory creating something evil.

As I clenched the doorknob to a rigid turn, my back opened from my ass to my head. That was the cut… But the wind behind the cut followed with a barbaric gust.

Ssskkkkkktttttt!

"Aahhhh!!" I bolted across the suite and crashed into the living room floor.

Ka-Flllooooommm!!!!

Rolling from my back, I crawled over the floor. While squeezing the drive in my nightgown pocket, my phone rung in the distance.

Crane's Residence

With the phone to my ear, I wept while pacing the floor.

"This mailbox is full and is no longer excepting messages. Goodbye. Loser."

I snatched the drawing from the wall and put it in my coat pocket. Then, out of frustration, I called again.

Suddenly, someone answered the phone.

"Hello!" I shouted as the phone heated up. "Canieya! This getting out of hand. You need to…Shhhiitttt!!" I hollered, dropping the phone.

The device bubbled and boiled like magma. I backed into the door, fidgeting with the locks as the phone melted through the floor. With fear in my eyes, I charged out of the house, slamming the door behind me.

But then, my eyes fastened to the sight across the street…

The first assassin crushed my phone into particles as he spoke in an unknown tongue.

That last cut was bad. Really bad. The blood was immense. It wouldn't be long before I bled out.

Was I dying?

Suddenly, my urge to live returned with a boost of adrenaline that I didn't expect.

My bleeding slowed and my pains vanished.

Something's up with me.

It felt like I was on crack.

My eyes batted to a visual crisp. Then I noticed the keys to my car on the floor next to the duffel bag of arsenal.

Stumbling to my feet, I yanked up the keys and the duffle bag. Then I hurtled over the couch in front of the balcony and ducked behind it.

I tied the keys up into the strings of my gory nightgown. Then I equipped myself with two AR-15s from the duffel bag.

My blood painted the floor as I peered around the couch to see the assassins entering the living room.

They're coming for me…

I ducked back behind the couch thinking, why the agents in the hall haven't responded?

"I'm going to yank your spine from that incision." The second assassin's foxy voice didn't have an accent. She sounded more like a computerized recording.

"Fuck you, bitch!!" I hollered while loading the weapons.

Then the pair spoke to each other again in a voice that I couldn't interpret—and I speak five languages. Six with Ebonics.

From behind the couch, I popped up firing.

The hollow points wrecked the room as the second assassin deflected the bullets with her bladed nunchakus. She fled back into the kitchen as her counterpart ran up the wall, darting right for me.

My aim was impeccable. I hit him at least ten times. But the bullets bounced around the room. As the shells chimed against the floor, the ninja jumped from the wall, swinging his sword.

Ducking his attack, I chucked the AR-15s, and grabbed the duffel bag.

As he landed, I caught him dead in the face.

Wham!

We both fell as the bag dropped from my waning grip. Slipping in my own blood, I dove for the shotgun in the duffle bag. But the bag hoisted into the air.

Crouching on top of the sofa was the second assassin. She stood, tossing the duffel bag across the room.

Fwumm!!

It crashed into the front door as her counterpart sat up.

Scampering over the floor, I rolled to my back. With my eyes fixed on the second assassin, I crab-walked backwards until my head banged against the patio door. Propping myself up against the glass, I panted slowly.

She squatted on top of the couch with her bladed nunchaku dangling menacingly…

The agony raced through my body as the blood drained from my back. My doubt rose high when the first assassin stood to his feet, shaking his head. Was I done for? Wait a minute… I should've been dead. What the hell's happening?

Just then, my pain resistance upgraded, and with ghostly aspirations. As I batted my eyes, my reasoning came clear. Everything pointed to the drive. Should've never opened that stupid shit. I leapt to my feet, and I rushed that ho- screaming in a rage!

She spun atop the couch with a roundhouse kick, crashing me through the glass door.

Blaasssh!

I plowed through the balcony railing like a bulldozer through a damp Kleenex.

Gripping onto the metal railing with my good hand, I glanced to the ground below. Not a single soul was there.

The rail bolts began to give as it bent from my clumsy weight.

While gripping the drive in my nightgown pocket, blood covered my eyes. The gore dripped from my back and to the street below.

The second assassin stepped through the broken glass door and stopped about three feet away. Her counterpart stood within the darks of the suite. Blending with the eeriness, he moved with the shadows…

The bitch queen retracted the blades into her dense nunchakus. She then put them into a holster on the back of her chunky belt.

"I forgot to tell you about Layian telepathy. Ms. Lawson, it is an extremely old form of mental telepathy that spawned from the depths of Tierun. Its reach became infinite as it is widely used… By my kind," she explained as I dangled from the rail.

"Of course, it is not that useful when a foe possesses the same skill of a greater caliber. But, to the simple-minded, it could prove to be… How should I say… Very effective. Here. I'll give you an example," she muttered, like a bitch-ass snake.

Her robotron voice left me disturbed beyond reason. But I refused to believe in aliens, and I wasn't about to let go of this railing. 'Cause Bookie… The thought of her encouraged my every sense of motivation.

"Szexta," she uttered with her vile voice.

And with ease, my index finger lifted from my closed grip.

"Agh!" I stammered as I tried to clench my fist, but a pain rendered me incapable. The agony was so appalling, not even I would care to endure.

"Exteq," the witch whispered.

Then, my middle finger lifted, loosening my grip even more.

"Oh God," I replied, glancing to the street below.

Slowly I lifted my eyes, gazing at my hand as if it was guilty of betrayal. But that pain came twice as fast and with no remorse.

My grip slipped as I returned to a resting dangle.

While peering at the street, then to my failing hand, police sirens blared from a far. Then, that foul-fuck bitch added with a threatening tone…

"Zxqvs."

Right then, all my fingers lifted from the railing. It was crazy, 'cause it felt like my hand was still intact. And all because of the curses spilling from that cunt's ratchet mouth.

But from the dark expelled my desire to devour.

My eyes batted with a fiery zeal.

I blossomed enough 'juice' for one last ride.

One last explosion of good…

CHAPTER: 17

A Wave Goodbye

Crane's Residence

Tom and his family stood in their yard, looking shot out. Everything was getting odd and creepy…like his wife. Her namaste-lookin' ass.

"Shh. Here he comes now,' Vera whispered as I approached.

Tom took his keys from his pocket as I sprinted across the street yelling, "Tom!"

"Oh, so we friends again," he shouted as he stood next to his car.

"My phone melted through the floor," I mumbled from the edge of his yard.

"Must've been calling too much," Vera blurted as we stared each other down.

"You wanna look," I sassed, gesturing over to the house. "'cause I can show you."

"Please do!"

"It's like lava."

"Derrick!!" Tom interrupted. "… I'm sorry. Crane, right? Look man, the whole neighborhood feels your loss. Believe me… We're all mourning with you and I'm willing to help as much as I can. I'm sure Canieya would, too. Where the hell is she, by the way?"

"Probably somewhere hanging from a balcony," I replied. "Have you spoke to her?"

"My. Phone. Mellll-ted, through the **floor**."

"Hey… I believe you…," Tom whispered as he clenched his keys. "Its like that doughnut. That hole in the sky."

"You ever heard of a Project Rapture?" I asked.

"Ugh… Let me see. Besides the rapture mentioned in the Bible, nope! Nothing else comes to mind."

"What about a hit list?"

"Political bodies and organized gangs use them to keep track of kills," Tom replied as his daughter grabbed his leg. "Man, can't believe you beat up your own house. Oh, hun!" Tom shouted. "Mr. Crane says thanks for towing Okani's car."

Vera sneered with hate. My eyes began to water as I dropped my head in guilt.

"We were just heading to the supermarket," Tom said as he tinkered with his keys. "You wanna come with? Grab some snacks or something? Or did we forgive each other already, or not? 'Cause I think we did. Damn sure feels like it."

That's when I felt horrible. Wallowing in my own prejudice, I hated myself. Maybe I had been cheated of my right to be human. But regardless of the macabre, and the unexplainable anomalies, my history replicated itself with no remorse. And realistically speaking… I'd lost my will to live…

"Hey, champ?" Tom cried as I turned away in tears. "Hey!"

"Let him go," Vera demanded as she opened her car door.

"Yeah," Tom replied. "Crane!"

Just then, I stopped as Tom skipped across the street. "This may not be any of my business, but… Are you on a hit list?"

With fear in my eyes, I peered over my shoulder and whispered, "That's *why* she's dead."

Tom hesitated as I walked with alertness to my car. "Holy shit," he stuttered as I opened the door. "Her bullet was for you."

Then I glanced over at him and his family, as they watched with dissimilar expressions. Tom and I stared into each other for a moment. Then I abruptly sat in the car, slamming the door in anger.

At a menacing speed, I fired out of my driveway as Tom scurried into the street.

"Hey!" he shouted as I flung the gear in drive. "Don't do nothing stupid!"

Before I fled off to my quietus, I peered into the rearview to see Tom's daughter waving goodbye. Little Tela cut my anger in half.

Tom dropped his head as he carried his daughter back to the car. And for some odd reason, his wife was still standing in the driveway, watching me. That's when I caught a glimpse of a badge clipped to her belt.

Ah-ha!

See, I knew there was something about her. Her Russian lookin' ass. Seemed like she never smiled. Vera looked like she mowed over her parents with one of those old school lawn mowers.

You know the kind you don't have to crank?

Damn right. Her namaste-lookin' ass…

CHAPTER: 18

Cliff Jumping

Inevitably, the blanket of night fell. I heard more sirens than normal. But I grew curious by the hour. The interest oiled in my eyes, growing anxious to see what the dead see… The sight of the afterlife and the ironic zing of death… by which, I had been conquered.

Matony won.

Downstate New York
The Palisades

With thirty minutes left in the day, I found myself parking next to a breathtaking cliff, that stood over five hundred feet above the Hudson River.

With the car still running, I stared over the Palisades. Then I put the car in park and emptied my pockets into the driver's seat. With haste I marched to the rear of the car and grabbed my gas can from the trunk. I doused the inside and the outside of the car down. Then I took the lighter from my pocket. Dithering in doubt, I flicked the lighter to a flame and I tossed it into the car. The vehicle ignited.

Bbboooooommm!!!!

The car exploded as I trucked toward the cliff. Staring over the setting, I psyched myself up. My timing grew accurate. Then my perception of thoughts left, and I waited no longer.

Suddenly I sprinted to the edge, and I jumped with all my might. Gravity came to my aid as I fell without screaming, without tears.

As my hearing ceased, the solid cold winds battered against my body, pushing my organs to my back.

All my problems were over. No more stress… No more bills… No more pains and fighting for respect… No more losing and struggling to get to a top that I would never obtain. No more Canieya. No more Bookie.

The ground was indistinct at first, but it formed into a plain of flat land. And as it approached, I felt even more, free.

My face detected the impact before I even reached the surface. But at two hundred feet from the ground, reality phased me. My consciousness returned. The only thing I could think of was: *Why haven't I hit the ground?*

Where was this sting of death that I so longed for?

The deviation crippled my brain to a mushy slush. Could it be? Am I so flicted that not even death would befriend me?

The air changed as I inhaled through my nose. Then that same hue that covered Okani's car surrounded me.

What the hell's happening here?

All I knew was that I wasn't dead, and I had somehow defied gravity.

But how? Gravity is the strongest force on Earth.

Then an ungodly feeling froze my body. And before I could utter a word, gravity's jerk inverted, and I was yanked with a wrench of straightness.

The monumental pain only lasted for a few milliseconds. But it was the worst ever… Veritably excruciating.

Imagine something ripping your skin off, only for it to stay fully intact…

CHAPTER: 19

When Clocks Elapse

My eyes opened to a dark abyss.

The air came thin and with an absurd odor. Then the flooring felt so dense. Its twinging, racking touch was worse than my flesh tugging.

Lying on my side, with my knees tucked into my chest, I wished for comfort. But I couldn't move. The gravity around me was too heavy.

My hands had been bound behind me. But these weren't ordinary handcuffs, and I'm very familiar with handcuffs.

Could this be hell?

Hell's supposedly hot. And I don't think demons would bind your hands.

"Hey!" a voice bellowed from the shadows.

My sight was so dull, it took me a moment to focus.

"Hey!" the voice shouted a bit louder.

Then, across the room, there appeared a figure, or a silhouette, of a man sitting against the wall.

"This hard-ass ground crazy, ain't it?" he said.

The more he spoke, the more his voice sounded familiar.

I peered deeper into the room.

"Don't struggle, Derrick. It only makes it worse," said

another voice.

This voice I instantly recognized.

"Quincy? What the hell's going on here?" I asked while looking to verify his face.

It was still too dark.

"God has called us," he cried.

"God, my ass! You gotta die to see dat cat. And we ain't dead, Q! Shit! This hard-ass ground!" the other voice yelled.

After hearing this voice again, I finally noticed his sporadic sense of dialogue. That could only mean one thing…

"Corey?"

"What's it to you? Oh! And Okani's here, too. She don't wanna talk to you, though," he said.

Mysteriously, all of my problems swept away. A tiny amount of light crept into the room as I captured a portion of Okani's face. I could feel her essence. Knowing that she was here wiped the slate clean.

"Egh! I dare you to stand up," huffed the speedster.

"Corey, why must you be so divisive and tricky?" asked the sweetest of voices.

"Okani???" I shouted. "Baby, is th—"

"Baby?!" Corey interrupted. "She ain't yo' damn baby!"

"I'll punch your face off right now!"

"Oh yeah?"

"Guys?" Quincy inserted as my skin tightened from anger.

"Come get me! Jackass!" Corey screamed. "Come on over here and catch this L!"

Okani just sighed as my spiritual tank filled with hate.

"Get the molasses outcha' panties, hard card!" the speedster retorted. "You move slower than a Walmart check-out! Get that ass over here!"

I was so furious that I started to stand. The odd weight of this room trounced my quads so that it seemed as if I was squatting a thousand pounds.

"AAAAgaaaaagggghhhhh!" I screamed as I reached an upright position.

My legs and hips shook uncontrollably.

"Holy shit…," mumbled the speedster.

Then I felt my skull, neck, and spine collapsing into one another.

Abruptly, I fell to the ground, yelling and vomiting.

"Why'd you do that, Corey?" Okani asked.

"He fucked up my gym and he stole money out of my swear jug! Damn menace to society!" the Speedster wailed. "Plus, I wanted to see if he could do it."

"Which is odd, 'cause neither of us could get to our feet, let alone stand," Quincy pondered.

"Yea, but he did," said the speedster. He stared at me as I continued to scream in the background.

"You didn't have to tease him, Corey," Okani insisted.

"Whatever yo! That's petty. Ya' dig? I wanna know what's on the other side of these hard-ass walls," said the speedster.

"Derrick?" Okani purred. "Are you okay?"

"Breathe through your nose," Quincy urged as I struggled to regain my composure.

"Sit up straight," the goddess demanded.

"Yeah, man. Sit like me, with your legs straight out. The pain will subside," Corey noted.

Breathing through my nose, I struggled to sit up. "It hurts!"

"I'm coming over there," whispered Okani.

She fell to her side and then onto her back. She used her legs and shoulders to scoot her body over to me. She moved fluidly and with ease, like a worm or a slug. I was amazed at how she defied the room's overly dense interior and injurious gravity.

She curled up beside me, aligning my head with her midsection. I grew a bit nervous when this happened.

"Smell me...," she whispered into my ear.

"Hey! Hey! What y'all doing over there?" growled Corey.

Her aroma calmed my troubled state. The pain was still there, but just not as potent. That's when I fell in love with Okani, all over again. "Vera had your car towed to the house." I spoke.

"Aw… I love Vera. Tell her I said thank you."

"Sure thing."

"You always doing some crazy shit," the speedster uttered.

"Hush, Corey. It's working," she replied.

"Bookies dead."

"What?" Quincy shouted.

"You mean the little girl you brought to the house?" The speedster asked.

"Oh no… the little queen. She was so young." Okani whimpered. "What happened?"

"I'm so sorry for your loss." Quincy sobbed.

"Yeah man. Sorry about your loss," Corey said. "You know I pick on you because I like you."

"This is the work of God," Quincy blurted with tears in his eyes.

"Ol' Father Harmon. Still holding up that blood-stained banner," Corey inserted.

"We've been…abducted," cried the clergyman. "By

aliens…"

"And we bout to die, too," Corey said. "Humans don't come back from abductions."

"End your negative spout, brother. No one's going to die," Okani softly insisted.

"You sure about that?" the speed demon asked. "Huh? How many times you been abducted and lived to talk about it?"

"True," Quincy grumbled. "We don't know what's about to happen. This is a fact that no one wants to accept. But it's happening to us. We should all be afraid."

"Damn right! I'm 'bout to shit my pants now. The only thing holding it in is this hard-ass floor." Corey chuckled.

We all laughed, including me, in all my watered-down pain.

Okani giggled. "You're disgusting, Corey."

"Always finding comedy in the storm." The clergyman laughed.

"This shit inevitable. Ya' dig? Might as well be happy. I can't wait to see what they look like." Corey motioned with his head as his lips trembled. "So, are we in a spaceship or a building?"

"It's hard to tell," Quincy muttered.

"Anybody got a watch or cell phone?" I painfully asked.

"Everything mechanical or technological is gone," Okani answered. "They took my purse, too."

"Yeah, man. I put my cell phone on vibrate when I realized I was being abducted. Didn't want to piss 'em off, you know?" said the speedster.

"How long have you guys been here?" I asked.

"Feels like about ten minutes," Corey answered. "I still got food from the football game sitting on my stomach. That's what…um 'bout to shit in my clothes once I —"

"Ten minutes?!" I yelled.

"Why?" Quincy asked.

"You guys have been missing for days."

"Our clocks elapsed" Okani whispered.

KCllung!

A heavy clang of opening locks jammed our eardrums. And the sizeable fear of our hardship followed behind a dazzling light, blinding us completely.

Something grabbed Okani and slid her violently over the floor.

Croom!

She crashed into the wall with a deafening grunt. The speed of the jolt must've killed her.

The beings greeted us swiftly, entering the coarse room.

I felt them and their aura, or their spirit. Whatever it was, it was strong, extraordinarily strong, and unpleasant. It became a vocal attack, and without them even speaking. We were rendered immobile.

They came directly over to me. Despite my need of a body cast, they grabbed me anyway, one by each of my shoulders.

Thucc!

My constraints dropped from my wrists, thudding to the coarse floor.

They lifted me up to my ass, and all my pains disappeared. In a sense it was sort of like magic. It was almost angelic in nature how my cure came from their touch alone.

They dragged me like a couple of savages. And I felt more helpless than domesticated cattle.

Father Harmon and the Dunlos grew smaller and smaller with every step my couriers took. This extended stare of mine widened with hysteria as the cell door began to close. Corey squirmed over to Okani, while Quincy prayed like mad. But soon they were all ingested by the inky gloom of the wicked, unholy cell.

CHAPTER: 20

The Hall Drag

The sounds of alien mischief jammed the foggy atmosphere. The noises were unexplainable and hypnotically entrancing. And making eye contact with my escorts was virtually impossible.

There were thousands of engines, machines, and instruments, small to grand in size, and in colors that never existed. In a startling fashion did this alien science merge into the walls of this massive hall. But I was in so much shock that I couldn't look at just one thing. My head was on a swivel.

There was one machine that caught my eye. Its buttons and various parts were moving, shifting, and sometimes merging with its own parts. By the time I looked away from this machine, it had become an entirely different piece of gadgetry. My eyes grew heavy from watching this massive machine for too long. But just as I began to doze off, fear locked my eyes wide open.

We were approaching a bisecting hall.

Upon turning into the hall, I faced a large opening. It appeared to be an oversize holding cell. I saw a creature sitting cross-legged in the middle of this room. He sat with his back facing me. The creature wasn't bound or restrained at all. And the door to this room was wide open. My carriers could not tell because they were facing the opposite direction, or maybe they didn't care. Suddenly, the creature's head lifted.

Its body resembled that of a human male. His skin was

very clean, silky, and black as the night sky. He had arms and legs just like me. But atop of his head were a pair of antennae. They stood straight into the air with small, dark yellow buds at the ends. They were very thin, almost like strands of hair. Then there were two red lines stemming over the top of his head and down his back. This being had no hair, but his body was well defined. Muscles on top of muscles and way beyond the normal human fascia. I could tell they were heavier in density, even from a distance.

His muscles were moving and traveling in every direction. Now, by human means, this engrossing feat was impossible. But the creature seemed to be doing this on his own.

His pecs inched around his back as his trapezius shifted over his shoulders and settled in his chest area. His obliques swiveled around his back. They shifted down while another set of abs toggled from under his chest cavity. His biceps, triceps, and forearm muscles all advanced up and down his arms. And this odd movement did not trouble the creature at all. He must've been using it as a workout. Or some form of meditation.

All in all, I was terrified. And concerned. Because his cell door was wide open. I wasn't sure if the being was a threat or not, but he had a masterful, godlike feel about him. The more I stared, the less I understood.

Finally, his head turned all the way around his neck. His face was sleek and nearly vacant. And his eyes where as black as his skin. But those sinister red lines grew from his eyelids, and over his forehead. With paper-thin lips and no nose, the creature looked to be just as surprised.

When we made eye contact, I couldn't turn away. Somehow, I was mentally trapped.

Without opening his mouth, he spoke demonically…

"Co—fi—oo—su—naa."

The sound was terrifying.

This was no ventriloquism. I had never heard a voice transmit without the use of a vocal box. So, of course, my tough exterior shattered. The action sent my mind into a damaging flummox. Before I could yell for help, the creature vanished, leaving me with thousands of already entangled stimuli. That's when I noticed the room that he had occupied. The walls were riddled with alien faces, mysterious eyes, and puzzling mouths.

This profound, and almost liberating, drag down the hall came to an end as we approached another passageway. And, from my view, the width of the flooring had tripled in size.

My carriers sat me on the dense floor while speaking in an unknown dialect. This language was quite different from that of the black-skinned creature.

What was happening?

Then I noticed that one of my carriers was only a huge blob of goo and tentacles. He was extremely scary and hideous.

A large set of doors opened, and a host of different voices followed with numerous other sounds that traveled briefly through the massive corridor. This was only a prelude of what was yet to come.

A pair of heels echoed through the hall as another being walked over to me.

My eyes wandered up to visually capture… a *woman*?

She was beautiful, just like a human beautiful. She had a mild complexion with a noticeably clear and almost ceramic appearance to her skin. She was a brunette, and her hair was wound up in a silky cloth material. Her clothing was different and costly looking. It was rugged and dark, like gothic attire.

She reached out to my face and grabbed my lips. She held them firmly for a moment as she dug into my psyche. Her hands were ridiculously hot with gears and wires turning within her fine skin.

"Speak human," she demanded as she let me go.

While scrambling for words, I honestly didn't know what to say. 'Cause this gorgeous woman spoke in English.

"What is your name?" she asked.

"Arlo," I replied

"Your full name."

"Arlo Tempest Crane," I quickly rattled off as she looked over my head.

She gestured upward, and my carriers lifted me from the floor. They sat me on an exceptionally clean and thoroughly sanitized surface. It was a cold table and way more comfortable than the ground below.

"I'll take it from here!" yelled a gruesome and degraded voice.

The gorgeous woman and my carriers all walked away as a supreme silence grew. Even the noise from the machines silenced.

But I still couldn't move.

The drama and anticipation of what was coming drove me mad. But all I could do was wait…

A fragment of time passed, then another being approached slowly, coming to my side. What I witnessed should've killed me. And I didn't want to believe it, but I had to.

This being seemed to be made of wood and or possibly ancient tree bark. His facial features were of human descent, and so was his skeletal frame. This wooden man was covered in tattoos, or maybe they were engravings of some kind. He was nearly naked except for the dingy loincloth that wrapped about his pelvic region. The biggest kicker of all (even though this man was predominantly composed of wood) was that this being had no legs or arms. He had nothing to support or to hold up his body. He mysteriously and mind-bogglingly floated in the air, gracefully defying gravity.

Over and under the wooden man did I search. There must be some type of explanation, or some form of assistance supporting him. There was no way he was just floating like that. It had to be wires.

He was extremely ugly, old, and just as horrifying as astonishing. But I continued to analyze the wooden man. He, at the same time, scrutinized my wandering eyes.

"Your globular organs do not deceive you," said the wooden man as he floated closer toward me. "There is only more mystery to this comprehension. I am the beginning of all ends—the start of your humanity's finish line. I am the physical embodiment of several thousand overlapping realities. The god who reigns over gods."

"Are you Jesus? You're Jesus, aren't you?" I asked with caution.

The wooden man dropped his wrinkly head and giggled. "No… But he's here, in the east wing. We're meeting for tea later."

His black starry eyes were piercing like small daggers. But what the wooden man said next trumped every card in my deck. "…Humanity…your poor humanity. You have become a part of something so grand that it'll make supreme beings look like scavengers, vagabonds. I know a deity whose job it is to create suns for several microcosms. Your humanity is in a toddler's stage.

"Every continuation, every universe, being, super or divine extraterrestrial response, decisions, and actions all stem from us. Every creation, TV show, belief system or book, fiction or nonfiction, graphic novel or comic, has its place because of us.

"Everything you have ever known answers to us on a mental scale that you may never grasp. At least not on this side of reality. But you, my friend...you have been elected by Arola and a group of important celestials," his expression grew serious. "And *I,* am their daddy."

All I ever learned came to an end. My mind opened like a bottle under pressure. It was then when I realized how vast space and its possibilities had become.

Man, I was in big trouble.

Suddenly, an image projected itself into my head. The wooden man was there in my thoughts, standing just as he was. Only this time, he had arms and legs. He reached out to shake my hand. In return, I grasped his old wrinkly palm.

His grip was intense.

My hand was extending out, firmly shaking his invisible hand. This connection was so real, even though the man was a floating quadriplegic. Somehow, my imagination or conscious mind had vanquished my physical existence. And for that short moment, my thoughts became my actuality—my world in realistic perception. How palpable could this be? This mental impression?

"I am Guitussami," he grumbled while firmly shaking my hand. "but you can call me Colonel G."

CHAPTER: 21

Change of Plans

The journey through this massive spacecraft lasted forever.

Colonel G explained so much to me until I began to view my skin's solidarity from an entirely different aspect. By his terms, humanity was obsolete or too young in our technological advancements.

The most interesting story he shared was how he lost his limbs. Plainly, Colonel G was so old that his archaic limbs became too heavy. One day, they simply fell from his body.

But Colonel G had access to all of his brain. He was so immersed in wisdom and knowledge that he understood reality. He knew how it all worked. He could've easily reattached his limbs just by telekinesis. But the ancient titan simply didn't need them anymore. Now, his Layian telepathy completes the task that his limbs once did, and with greater ease. This explained the handshake and the weightless floating of his body.

I, and the table I was on, had been following alongside the colonel for the entire length of our trip. Dozens of questions filled my head, but the colonel was so many steps ahead of me. Before I could ask any thing, he would already be answering. The awesomeness of this communion should've killed me several times over. Yet something sustained me. Indefinitely.

"We have a different plan for you," the colonel expressed as he gracefully floated beside me and my hovering table.

The archaic being and I had begun to bond. I thought of the quadriplegic as a friend.

"Now, the beings here are quite distinct and brash in spirit. Don't expect this gentle nature. You will undergo a horrific experiment that will utterly change your entire chemical makeup from the inside out. And then, you will die," he explained as we slowly floated to a very large mechanical door. "We figured you wouldn't mind the company of death since you were so eager to meet her. An odd being she is…"

Colonel G hovered ahead as my table stopped a few feet away. He stopped next to a large device by the door.

Mechanical noises and computer-like voices emitted from the device. Suddenly, the massive doors opened, and a bright light pierced through.

I laid behind Colonel G, watching closely as he peered hesitantly over his shoulder. "You are no more…," he whispered as he floated to one side.

The suspended table and I drifted slowly into the light.

"Hey! Wait a minute!" I shivered in fear glancing about as I eased by the colonel and into the hallway.

Colonel G dropped his head as the tail end of the floating table finally passed through. My head whipped around to see a figure in the distance. Whatever it was, it was moving fast.

As the figure ran straight toward me, I saw that this was a doctor, wearing a long white lab coat. He stopped—well, he slowed momentarily—beside the floating table.

"I'll be right with you," he said as he dashed behind me.

"Heyyy! What the fuck!" I screamed while scrambling to get off the table.

Still invisibly bound, I calmed myself enough to eavesdrop on the conversation behind me.

"The Feuler? Did **what**?!" the colonel yelled.

The doctor spoke in English when talking to me, but when he spoke to Colonel G, he used a strand of syllables and sounds.

"Switch the procedure!" the colonel ordered.

The doctor spoke again in such erratic noises. His voice turned into a cybernetic computer full of clicks and motherboard surges.

"All right! All right!" Colonel G shouted as my table stopped drifting. "This is the last time."

The doctor calmly approached the side of my floating bed, breathing wildly. "Hi. I'm Doctor Phlaxlur. It's a pleasure to meet you," he huffed, holding out his hand.

"The fuck?! Doc?? You're the guy from Dunlo's house!" I said as the doctor snickered.

Mysteriously, my constraints lifted, as I reached out to shake his hand while still bound to this floating bed of damnation. "What's about to happen to me, Doc?"

"Ohh man…," he muttered. "Good question. Let's just say that this is one of three processes. This entire procedure may take about three years. Or at least as we measure time. That's about… Let's see, three Earth days, maybe."

"What? Holy fuck!" I hollered, but Doctor Phlaxlur was laughing.

Struggling again to free myself, I glanced around to see Colonel G in the distance, still floating at the main entrance of the hallway.

"Now, now. Let's not wake the neighbors," Phlaxlur whispered as he stepped in front of my sight of the wooden man. The doctor giggled as he pushed me deeper into the raw white light.

CHAPTER: 22

The Fact Matter Room

Without the interruption of dreams, I woke up feeling restored.

My eyes opened to a dimmed light and another doorway that only reflected my own mien. This door was so huge that I didn't think it could open. But the door was already opening, and I had no time to prepare.

Dr. Phlaxlur hurried to the front of the table. His alert and giggly demeanor changed into a form of fear. Then, with his back turned toward me, we entered through the doors.

The appearance of this room did not aid in my comfort.

Transparent holograms, hovering DNA strands, molecules, atoms, and particles were splayed over this magnificent corridor. I saw over several hundred floating monitors and rows and rows of advanced devices. They were all controlled by thousands of scientists. This visual extended for so long that the flooring and the basic structure of this chamber began to spiral. I couldn't believe my eyes.

This unfathomable hall was not in a stir. The scientists were pretty composed and very orderly about their conductive nature.

Dr. Phlaxlur walked over to a nearby wall that contained a built-in filing system. He took a small green disk from the wall and stuffed it into his pocket. I had no idea what he or the other doctors were working on, but it had to be big.

The doctor walked in a bit farther, and I caught a glimpse of a very peculiar floating diagram. I wasn't sure, but it seemed to resemble some sort of formula.

As the enigma presented itself to the massive body of experts, they all stopped in their footsteps. Everything froze as if they were studying this closed book. One alien reached into its lab coat, and a digital hologram about the size of a small rectangle appeared beside his head.

This small rectangle was filled with symbols that I didn't recognize. The alien single-handedly typed into the rectangle while still studying the hanging formula. Several other scientists began to do the same thing. They all acted as if the doctor and I weren't even there.

Suddenly, the room went crazy.

The scientists switched from one station to the next. One scientist pulled out an archaic laptop, which was very strange.

Doctor Phlaxlur was still pushing me on into the intersecting hall, which sat adjacent to the oversized doorway.

But I couldn't take my eyes off this extremely long hall.

I peered through the transparent formula only to capture the sight of another being far off in the room. Even though the being sat at a great distance, I was still able to discern this image.

The being rested at the end of this elongated hall. It was a man, and he sat in a massive chair or a throne full of artistic engravings, diamonds, gold, rubies—you name it. All the precious jewels and elements of matter that I knew and never knew were infused into this seat. But this man was so spectacular that his mighty chair was of no comparison.

His presence was immeasurable.

As I gathered myself, I saw that this man appeared to be of human descent. He was shirtless, but his wrist and ankles were decked out in gauntlets and exotic bracelets. His physique was just like mine, but his face was intricately masked. I couldn't make it out. The mask was so sharp and classy that it grasped all of my attention.

The being lifted his head slowly, and as he did, my eyes traveled up to his scalp. And that's when I noticed his hair. It was a deep black bush that extended high into the ceiling of this grand room. His hair split up into two large pieces that fed into a couple of rings about the size of roller coaster loops. The rings had been coupled to the left and right corners of the ceiling.

His hair filled the entire center of the rings. And behind this impressive being was a field of black grass. But the more I looked, the more I realized this field was not made of grass. It was more of his hair, expanding beyond an even more incalculable space. It looked like a black ocean.

Just as I was about to scream, Phlaxlur stepped in front of me, leaned up to my ear, and whispered, "Don't look in his eyes."

"Whaaaa… Who… *is* that?" I stuttered in fear.

Phlaxlur didn't say anything else. He just double tapped the edge of my floating death bed.

The hovering table turned down the adjacent hall.

Time elapsed…

CHAPTER: 23

Time Buckle Thesis

Phlaxlur stopped by a wall as he pulled out a flat green disk, about fourteen inches in diameter. He immediately typed into it as the disk floated up beside him, projecting holograms into the air.

"Doc…who was that in that big-ass chair?" I bellowed with fear.

Phlaxlur kept walking beside me, typing into the disk.

But to my eyes, those guys were extraterrestrial celebrities! That man must've been God.

"Doc!" I screamed.

The table stopped as he looked away from the floating disk and pointed with sternness.

"We speak not of him… Never!" he yelled, and I shut up, gulping a bunch of spit.

The doctor continued to point and stare into my face. "Just don't look in his eyes," he ordered while turning back to type into the green hovering disk.

Phlaxlur glanced to the table, then up to me. "What'd you do?" he asked.

"Huh," I replied.

Just then, the table started to float again.

Phlaxlur glared into me for a moment before he resumed typing into the green disk.

Now, I didn't want to wonder about what I saw, but that wide opening behind that significant being was just too big. Was I gazing off into a chain of monstrous black mountains? How is that possible when the black mountains originated from his scalp? What was even more amazing was that all of this was contained within one large planet of a room.

"How big is this ship?" I mumbled to myself.

"Ship? You've been off that ship for a while now," Phlaxlur interjected.

"I don't remember the landing."

"Of course… You, like most, fall asleep during the Time Buckle. Besides, you wouldn't have noticed anyway. It's quite seamless."

That's when I noticed that my very notion of time had been modified greatly. "What's a Time Buckle?"

"The Time Buckle is a thesis that hundreds of scientists, including myself, have explored and later interpreted," Phlaxlur answered. "However, it can only be explained by the complete breakdown of time.

"But here, there is no time, only coordinates and light-based formulas known as Layian cycles. This asteroid is just too massive. It's a compilation of overlapping galaxies. There are too many zones to govern, and they all have a standard of placement. Layian cycles locate each placement. They erase your idea of time.

"There are only a few here that can equate the many zones and convert them into cosmic events. I'm familiar with some of the conversions. Planets are simple to equate. Our light equations tally every spin, even down to the teeniest, weeniest rotation.

"But doing that for the Layo Galaxy? Ha! Not even I could do that completely." Phlaxlur chuckled. "We don't spin here."

I wasn't expecting that answer. But I did opt-in for the pop quiz. "You said that we are on an asteroid?"

"Yes," Phlaxlur replied. "And it's about the size of several galaxies congealed together."

"…If this asteroid is so big, how do you commute?"

"Great question, Crane. Every large spacecraft moves at the speed of light here. Then the Unitran, our version of a locomotive, covers over sixty percent of the galaxy. The monorail can travel ten times faster than light, providing us with quicker routes for longer travels," he said. "Then we have TPD(s). They zap us to certain areas of the asteroid within a matter of seconds."

He stopped typing into the disk. Then he turned to look at me with those pixelated eyes. "I keep forgetting. You haven't seen this place."

"That *is*, you!"

"What do you mean?" the doctor quizzed.

"You're Corey's doctor! Man, I know you. How da hell you get out here?"

Phlaxlur giggled. "That wasn't me exactly. In this galaxy, I'm known for the creation of a portable chamber, surgically implanted and primarily used to create weapons out of high-definition lasers and pixels. Let me tell you, the internal CPU contains a script for creations of solid image conversions, sent to a miniaturized system of conveyor belts. The chamber instantly designs and stitches any weapon together by mixing solid pixels with…"

Phlaxlur paused.

"Sorry, got wrapped up in my accomplishments. But the guy you saw was only a replica, with the same aptness for creation. You see, I also found a way to duplicate myself, so there is one of me in every solar system the Symbassy guzzles. It's all part of the project."

"Project Rapture."

The doctor looked concerned. "How do you know about Project Rapture?"

"My old lady… she told me. She found a hit list and some triple beam crazy shit designed for cosmic conquest or something."

"What planet are you from again?"

"… Why?" I stammered as the doctor's smile wiped away. "You must work for them?"

We glared into each other just before he typed into the disk again. "Planet Earth… uh-huh. Someone must've cracked the drive. No big deal," he mumbled. "Problem solved." He then scowled. "Oh, due to the recent events of Space Void, your procedures will have to be staggered. You just stepped into a war."

"War?!"

"Yep! The Feuler fucked up everything." he explained as he typed into the disk. Then the device shrunk to the size of a dime and Phlaxlur placed it over his pupil. "Arola sanctioned the abductions. *And…* you shouldn't have stood up."

Finally, our long travel ended.

The floating death bed stopped in front of a stained door. My flesh tingled as my worry escalated, but there was nothing I could do.

Phlaxlur swiped his index finger against a small panel. The doors opened immediately.

A deep red mist of light emerged from the room. Phlaxlur

stood to the side as my floating bed filtered into the risky fog.

In a trice, two aliens snatched the bed in and the gory doors slammed shut.

CHAPTER: 24

Blood Space

My wrist shattered as I tumbled into the coarse room.

Klloomm!!

"I'm not resisting! I'm not resisting!"

Wham!

They slammed me violently onto another deathbed.

My floating table streaked off to a zap of light.

Zzzcccc!

Screaming from the throbbing fractures in my hand, I finally glanced at the black-eyed, big-headed, little gray aliens from Area 51.

"You're real," I whispered.

They didn't speak. They just kept handling me like crappy luggage.

Suddenly, I bolted stiff to the table.

"Agh!" I shouted as my invisible constraints resumed.

The thought of anal probing had me looking around neurotically.

This space was about as big as my house. But I couldn't understand the structure. The room had no sides. The corners just didn't fit the formation. This, of course, made no sense to me. The more I tried to understand the room, the more complex it became.

As my eyes wandered, I noticed another gory bed beside me. It sat next to a tub built into the coarse flooring. It was filled with entrails.

I turned away from the sight. Shaking wildly, I glared into the ceiling for relief. But there were so many sharp, menacing tools hanging there. The gizmos were attached to the ends of what I perceived to be a jumble of intestines, nerves, and spinal cords.

Shifting from the ceiling, I stared straight ahead. But androids moved about the room, century-old machines that hovered about the air. And with every stop the droids made, the computers in the walls would turn into a different type of equipment. This happened all over the room and high into the ceiling.

The technological overlay was so disturbing, that my mind could not grasp the makeup.

The aliens scuttled about the room, collecting their tools.

Then the door opened suddenly, and I looked over to see Phlaxlur. "I apologize for the excitement. Forgot to upload your procedure." He laughed.

The door shut fast as the computerized room finished adjusting.

Phlaxlur stood at the head of my bed. Facing me, he slid a disk into a crack in the wall. A diagram of circuits, images, and mathematical expressions filled the air. The entire room dimmed in its coloration, and a great calm followed as I marveled at this formulated chasm.

The small gray aliens pointed at the images, communicating in their native tongue. Doctor Phlaxlur joined in as he walked over, pointing to certain areas.

But I closed my eyes while listening to them quarrel. Really, I just wanted to die.

Then the door opened again, and everything stopped.

Everything.

Both aliens gawked at the door while Phlaxlur dropped his head, as if he knew who entered the room. It had to be someone of importance to stop these guys.

The suspense was overwhelming…

The door closed as I peered over to see Colonel G creeping in, hovering smoothly as usual. My heart leaped with joy.

He stopped and looked at the transparent diagram that had taken over this surgical blood space.

We were all stiff, even the little gray aliens.

While examining the images, Colonel G floated over to the wall behind me.

Alas, Phlaxlur whirled around, pointing sternly at Colonel G. "Tussami, don't you start this shit!" he yelled with a twitching hand.

Colonel G looked at the doctor. Then he looked over to

the slot in the wall, where Phlaxlur inserted the disk.

"Guitussami???" Phlaxlur shouted.

Colonel G had yet to respond, and Phlaxlur was still pointing as rigid as possible.

Suddenly, the entire diagram glitched. It happened so fast that I barely noticed. The only thing that gave it away was when Phlaxlur lifted his head to the ceiling. He closed his eyes and yelled, "…God! Damn it! Tussami…"

"He hates that," the colonel noted, peeping at me with a smirk.

"You do this every time!" Phlaxlur howled. "This is *my* procedure."

"Yeah, but it's *Arola's* project," the Colonel retorted as he floated over to Phlaxlur.

A tiny box ejected from the Colonel's midsection like a disk drive. "Use this in conjunction with the Gray Garden formula."

Phlaxlur snatched the box from his abdomen.

"Agh!"

"I'm sorry!"

"Just kidding." Colonel G smiled as the abdomen slit shut.

Phlaxlur leered at Colonel G, gripping the box firmly.

The big-headed aliens were just as lost as I was. The only difference was that I was about to die at the hands of these fools.

"Is that all?" Phlaxlur sassed. "Sir?"

"Yes…that is all," Colonel G replied as he turned to me.

He looked back to Phlaxlur and then sadly down to the ground.

Phlaxlur kept gawping, tapping the box against his hand as Colonel G floated in disapproval.

They looked worried. It must've been something serious to vex my company of aliens.

What could it be? What could possibly stew them?

"You may begin, doctor…," the Colonel instructed.

Phlaxlur tossed the box up in the air and caught it, shouting, "Awesome." He then whirled around to face the big-headed aliens. "Let's go, guys!"

Phlaxlur waited a second while they goggled with hesitation. Then he reiterated his joy for stardom in their native tongue and they all shot over to their devices.

Colonel G continued to stare at the ground as he began his slow exit.

"You leaving me?" I asked as he graciously passed with a concerned look on his face. The colonel kinda reminded me of Tom. But he was about to leave without saying anything else to me.

"Hey!" I shouted as my hand throbbed away.

The colonel didn't stop. He just kept floating by.

He reached the door and peered over his shoulder. "I have a meeting to attend," he finally answered.

The door opened quickly.

On the other side of the door stood two beings.

One of the beings resembled the black-skinned creature that I saw during my so-called *hall drag*. The only thing was that his skin wasn't black; it was gray with a hint of green speckles. His eyes were squinty with a blur of yellow and a pair of antennae sat atop his head. He was taller than me. And his heavy attire had an Earthly influence.

He had on a horrid, rust-orange bubble vest that reeked every time it moved. The odor was so bad, you could see it. He wore some dingy brown gloves, a pair of thick khaki cargo pants, and some… *Timbs?*

He also wore a long necklace that stopped about his midsection. The necklace came with a charm that looked like two exclamation points side by side. One upright, and the other upside down. This jewelry looked extremely costly. But what made the alien so quirky was that he had a toothpick in his mouth.

Now, the other being looked totally human. The sheik must've got into a fight with death and won by unanimous decision. He just looked so scruffy.

His skin was like brass and full of ancient scars, especially around his forehead. His hair was thick as lamb's wool. As a matter of fact, his beard looked as though hadn't been cut in forever. But his eyes were like balls of fire. And his hands stayed hidden within the sleeves of his old, dilapidated robe. And I may have been mistaken, considering the floor's density, but I believe this man was barefooted.

This was all hard to perceive. Each of these individuals were standing upright, oblivious to this cataclysmic force of extreme gravity.

"Is that him?" asked the horrid vest-wearing alien.

Colonel G nodded.

As the barefooted man peered in, the other alien took the toothpick out of his mouth. "Oh…he bout to get fucked up!" he blurted as Colonel G drifted out of the room.

"How about that tea?" the Colonel suggested as the doors shut.

"Somebody needs to bayz dey' ass," Phlaxlur whispered.

With a deep breath, I glanced into the ceiling. Just that fast, I forgot about the horror brewing above. My attention was redirected to the hologram overrunning the room.

My wrist ached anew.

Suddenly, the transparent diagram disappeared.

Doctor Phlaxlur flipped a nearby panel over to its opposite side. Then he pushed the panel into the wall, and the entire room flicked to a blue hue.

Phlaxlur spun around with a smile on his face, speaking in revelation. “Get ready.”

But before I could respond…

CHAPTER: 25

Gastropoda: Gray Garden
Part 1

* * *

Humid and brilliant was the sunny day as I sat on my front porch. Fresh out of rehab, I felt as if I won the battle against my crack addiction. So, in celebration, I decided to smoke a blunt.

My life was all right, I guess.

Mom left me the house in her will. And I didn't have any kids or girlfriends. It was just me and a few of my friends who were either still in high school or in college at the moment.

As time rolled by, I lit my blunt with several puffs.

Then somebody came speeding down the street, driving recklessly in nature. The guy who was riding shotgun rolled down his window. He sat on the door ledge, plucking an object from his mouth.

He spat the remains into the road and launched the item over to my house.

The object bounced against the door and then to my wooden porch, rolling under my rocking chair.

Pinching the blunt with my lips, I sat up in the old chair. And for a second, I couldn't figure out what it was. Then it hit me…

"Grenade!"

My adrenaline soared as I sprinted off the porch, spitting the blunt to the grass.

Fwwwwoooommmmm!!!!

The explosion shot me out of the yard, and I into the road.

And just like that, the entire neighborhood was in the streets. People were calling the police, while my neighbors approached me screaming as I laid on the ground. Peering over to the car as it sped away, I took a mental picture. Then I glanced over to my house—and right into the backyard. The whole front porch was gone.

The next thing I knew, my setting changed…

Early one morning, Bookie and I lounged at the kitchen table of my second home. She sat in front of me eating cereal, and I just sat there staring. She was only two or three. And at that time, she had changed my life so much that I lost my will to fight. I refused to put her in any danger.

Then Canieya walked into the kitchen.

She had just gotten out of the shower. She was wearing her favorite white house robe and her white stiletto mules with the fur at the top.

Her toes were always pretty, I mean... always— You hear me? And her calf muscles were so sexy. The way the back seam of her sheer white stockings traveled about the contour of her delicate, ladylike definition— Man!

She sure knew how to be a lady, so elegant and feminine.

She stood at that white refrigerator when she began to untie her house robe. With a short seductive look, she opened her robe to display her lingerie.

Our first kiss...was so...

The vision shattered quickly as Bookie's death interrupted my thoughts.

The man gripped Bookie about her tiny neck with one hand. And with his other hand, he held that chrome .357 Magnum.

The sound rocketed through my soul.

Blam!

***

Present Day | Somewhere in the Layo Galaxy

As the Magnum's blast waned, a rigid cold dispelled my dreamy state quivering me to stir…

My eyes opened as I laid naked on the ground, curled up in the fetal position.

An airy sound resonated through my eardrums.

My fear of standing grew, especially after what happened the last time. However, I had to get off this floor. My body temperature was dropping fast. My lips and teeth chattered out of control while my breath evaporated into the biting cold.

A hint of light came suddenly behind me.

My interest grew as I glared into the thermal emissions bouncing off the wall in front of me.

In the midst of my turning, I peered at the floor and the ceiling to see them full of circular vents. The walls were tall, maybe about twelve feet high. But the width of my space was only about six feet. The floor and the ceiling were both flat. The walls, however, were curved like a cylinder.

This wasn't the laboratory. And this cold and scary tube had me all to itself. Or did it?

"Hello!" I shouted.

No one responded.

While creeping over to the light, I ducked down to avoid the soft beam of illumination. Didn't want to trigger an alarm or something. But I had to see what was happening.

The light cured my irrational distress. But then I noticed a window in front of me.

My eyes leveled with the edge of the pane. And at this moment, I was highly interested in my developing perspective.

As I glanced around, the threat of the crushing force invaded my memory. That's when I recalled how bad it was, in that room with Q and the Dunlos. Damn, I miss Okani…

After a few seconds, my established belief of this altered gravity retreated from my thoughts. Maybe it took a nap or something. Yet, at the height of my anxiety, I stood.

"AAAAaaaaaggghhhh!" I screamed.

But then, I fell victim to a resplendent sight.

Through the window of my cold confines, I saw a magical and mystical setting. So harmonious and breathtaking. The logical coherence of this landscape took my mind hostage. This creation made Earth's splendor look sad. In comparison, Earth was the ghetto version of this planetary formation. For this developmental production, God would've required some aid. This beauty required days to perceive.

Hundreds of planets, distant stars, and beautiful sunsets trickled colors over fifty different waterfalls.

The bodies of water continued into infinity as the streams never ran dry. The elegant fall of rivers created showers of what I thought to be layers of water. But the liquid calmly traveled in a horizontal direction, only to rise and feed into another body. They traveled up into a space of no end. The ascending eminence repeated like steps on a ladder until the magnificent sight vanished into the colors of those stranger skies.

Equally intriguing as the escalating waters was the periphery around this water. Nothing contained it, not even a structured boundary. It flowed freely with no restraint. It had a mind of its own as if this impression of water-controlled gravity.

But I wouldn't put the abilities of this place beyond me. I

stared at this phenomenon for at least an hour before I even noticed the rest of my awakened surprise.

Amid spectacular fates, several misshaped moons, asteroids, and another host of stress-singing hues, colors that I couldn't grasp repeated. There were thousands of unforeseen colors influencing my perception. On one side of my gaze was a variety of reds. On another side was a form of orange. Then directly in the middle was a blend of the colors that all mimicked the saturations found on Earth. Into an incomparable distance, of beauty did this glory persist.

This image was as grand as anything I had ever seen.

Everywhere I looked, I was engulfed by more beauty.

As far as my eyes could discern, this beyond-pleasing sight repeated itself over and over. The view was so breathtaking that I began to cry. But under the frigid circumstances, my tears froze on production.

Stepping closer to the window, I cautiously reached out to the glass. The window rippled like waves in a puddle.

"Whhoooaaaa…," I mumbled as I stepped back, staring at my hand.

My wrist was like new.

As my stomach growled, I glanced over my confines and the glorious setting all at once. This was truly a reward of elegance before my moment of death.

"Where am I?"

Just then, a being floated directly in front of the capsule. This three-foot tall, computerized cylinder, moved with so much fluidity. A diagram popped up next to the being, while it accessed the holographic display. Then the diagrams zipped away, and the mechanical being jetted off into the glorious settings.

Glancing back over to the window, I looked down and couldn't see a bottom. There had to be some sort of explanation. While studying the area carefully, I walked to the far end of the window. This capsule of mine was attached to something larger. But to my other side, and in the distance, I saw another capsule attached to the side of a mountain. But no one was in there.

By now, my teeth were chattering so bad that I couldn't think straight. Stepping back from the window, I hugged myself, for the light brought me no warmth. With my eyes fixed on the heavenly sighting, I waited patiently for my bones to freeze.

All sorts of godly events were transpiring before me. The scenery excited me so much, my enthusiasm pushed me to exercise.

The urge to keep my blood moving, the urge to stay alive, settled in my gut. Eventually, I fatigued from dehydration. Plus, the small amount of sweat nearly froze me stiff.

My thoughts and my memories cycled through my brain at an extremely fast pace. Then they slowed to a stop as I felt myself passing.

"Fuuuccckkkkk…" I chattered. "Daddy's coming, Bookie. Daddy's coming…"

Suddenly, a lock turned.

Cunk!

At first, I denied the sound because I hadn't heard anything in a while. However, I scoped the scene, searching for whatever it could be.

Seconds later, the smell of my confines changed. The smell wasn't poisonous, but it was weird. This, of course, made my eyes wander.

Staring at the floor of my capsule, near the front just under the window, I saw it creep in… Some sort of…something.

This thing was about four inches in length and maybe about two inches in width, and it was moving slow.

Cautiously I stepped back as this thing became the center of my attention. Not even my setting, in its throne of immaculate landscape, could take my eyes away… This small persistent thing was so attractive that I forgot how cold it was.

"Hey!" I shouted as the thing stopped. Did it hear me?

Suddenly, a pair of proportioned antennae unfettered from the things' head.

"Wait! That's a slug," I said, while backing up from the mollusk. "Hey, fella… Now I don't wanna step on y—"

Just like that I was paralyzed, and I immediately developed an overpowering migraine.

The slug sat upright with its antennae erect.

"Aaaggghh!" I shouted with a frozen face of despair.

It was increasingly difficult to think. And every time I tried to move; my headache would get worse.

"Uuuuggghhhhh…," I mumbled in agony as the small slug wiggled through my toes.

It slid its way onto my foot, traveling slowly up my leg. The slug muscled over to the inner side of my thigh. Then it continued up the center of my back. The gastropod stopped on my shoulder before it scooted slowly up my neck, to my jawbone, and then along the side of my face. When it reached my earlobe, the slug hung like a heavy earring. Then it lifted itself into my ear canal. And there it waited and waited as I stood in torment.

Suddenly, the slug thrust itself into my ear. It felt like a table was being shoved into my head. My screams went insane.

But then my headache stopped, and my paralysis released.

I dug into my ear to retrieve the small slug, but I couldn't tell if it was still there or not. Suddenly, a violent internal pain erupted, and I went batshit crazy.

The gastropod made me delirious as I threw myself from wall to wall. Then I fell flat on my face, banging my head against the floor until it bled.

Then I rolled and kicked, jumped, and squatted. While grabbing my head, I fell to my knees, screaming to the top of my lungs until I ran out of air. Then, slowly, the pain ceased.

From my altered state, I shook uncontrollably. Then I wiped over my body fervidly to see if the slug was still there. I was delusional.

The blood on my face froze to a crust. As I scraped it away, my innards churned over inside me. Organs I never knew I had flexed and bent in ways that they shouldn't.

Breathing hectically, I fell lifelessly to the floor yelling, "Fuck!" As I curled up, my insides broke down and reassembled.

Then I experienced a bowel movement like none other, passing my own feces as well as several other objects.

My nose began to bleed. Then that slug inched out of my nasal cavity. It doubled in size as it slurped from one nostril and into the other.

"You! Fuck!" I hollered as I gulped down the slug.

Suddenly, the pain stopped. But I could still feel the slug swimming back up my esophagus and into my brain.

With my hands propped on my knees, I rested on my feet, shaking my head and rocking back and forth.

Just then, another slug came from under the window. This one was much smaller than the first. But as this slug trailed in, so did another one. Then another. And another. And another followed from under the window.

"Oh shit! Fuck no! NO! NOOOoooo!" I hollered as a host of slugs crawled through the floor vents. "Shit!" I yelled while squabbling over this sluggish onslaught.

Then, from above, I felt rain, or what I assumed to be rain.

And with my dumbass mouth wide open, I glanced into the celling. Dozens of slugs dropped clean into my throat.

They burrowed into my pores as I bleed from my mouth. Then a burning sensation covered my skin. My flesh began to cook. This must've been why it was so cold… The pain of this ungodly frying grew into a demonic nightmare.

My teeth fell from my gums, one by one, like salivating drops of drool. With my hands in front of me, I caught my nose as it slipped from my face.

All of my hair fell out. My penis and scrotum singed clean

off my pelvis. Then my fingernails and toenails oozed away, spewing like small faucets of running blood.

The slugs frolicked about as they battered their way into my bloodstream. They eventually filled the capsule with a slimy acidic trail. And I was literally waist-deep in this corrosive acidic mucus. As my voice box ruptured, I ran out of tears. My eyeballs cooked out of their sockets, and the last few inches of my God-known flesh melted into this cohesive bond. My muscles and nerves were completely exposed as my raw senses fried to a crisp.

Years into this skin conversion, a new encasing fused to my body. After reaching the pinnacle of this repulsive sludge, the acidic slime thickened to a concentrated mold. Insubstantially flawed, I became just as dense as the Layian asteroid. This transformation virtually wiped my memories cleaner than a reformatted drive.

In the end, there was no more Crane. My karma required so much back pay that *this* served as my only outing.

Man, I finally got what I wanted…

Thank You

Dear Reader,

Crane here!

I know, I know… I just died. Lucky for you, I recorded this message beforehand. And you've come a long way through space. How'd you get here?

Never mind that…

I love that there are *others* in outer space who enjoy taking that galactic trip away from it all. So…you wanna know what happens to Canieya? Well, get ready for Book Two.

Friends! Book reviews can do so much, especially for indie authors. In fact, every time you share a good review, an angel gets his wings…

That shit ain't true at all.

But feel free to leave an honest review on Amazon, Goodreads, or anywhere you find *Evolving Crane.* And if you enjoyed this book, tell your friends. Be sure to get together and draw up your own plot twist.

Welp, I'm off to finish dying…

You never know where evolution will take you.

For Correspondence:

Dave Welch

P.O. Box 6402

Macon Ga. 31208

www.itsdavewelch.com

Email me: adaptorstudio@gmail.com

Review Your Purchases (amazon.com)

Acknowledgments

First, I'd like to thank the higher being (God, the universe, or whatever you would like to label it). Second, I want to thank my mother and father for putting up with me and my crazy antics. Finally, I would like to thank all of my sisters, Joe, my brother, nephews, and all of their kids.

I want to thank all my friends and fans of the M.O.S. movement: Darnell, Eli, Barnum, "Frank Castle," Bernardo Gomez and the family, "Hater" Chris, "Black Gabby," Tron, Thoom, Pendergraph, Titus, Kurt, IP, "Ice-Man," "Homebwoi Fi," Lundi, Lance Darden (my nemesis), Alan Bardwell, Able Melody, Mike McGill, Tom Biondolillo, Tom Grant, Paul Orlando, Val, Bubby Mitchell, Q, Lathan, "Quan more time," Big Stephen Eakin and family, Big Gainey, Chris, Tyree, Red, Terri, C.B., Courtney Ruth, Matthew Baker, Cat and Monotone Cat, Big Hob, Jake Joe, Robert Evans, Nadine, Sky Wind, Damian, RTB, Mr. William Kingpop Floyd, Kius Scales, "Sloppy Flow," Big Perm, John Haze, Thomas Dunscombe, Aharon Eran Yashar'al, Huie, Taylor, Byron Johnson, "Big—Yeah" Brian Edwards, Gruel,

David Capoferri and the family, Chuck Lilly Jr., Omar, Vince White, Scott "Attkins," Thomas "Thanos" Marroquin, Jihad Griffin, Miz Dreekull, Cliff Hangerman, D.J. Hawk Cannon, D.J. Welch, Jeffery Scott, and all of those I missed. Thank you all for your support and your belief in me. This one's for you and for the soon-to-be fans of this new era in cartoon animation.

RIP Shenean and Carlos.

I love you, Data!

excerpt_ A

Evolving | **Crane**
Book 2|Archipus

A savage cut came from under the pod seat.

Chisz!

"AAaaagghhhh!!!" the merc screamed as his foot was clipped off, scattering blood over the monorail.

He fired wildly, wobbling to the floor.

The Feuler came out of nowhere, chopping into the man's head.

Bish!

He yanked out his butcher knife as the mercenaries fired.

Sparks of death zinged by as the Feuler split in two.

The firing stopped when the mercenaries lost sight of the deranged butcher.

They advanced forward slowly, stopping about eight pods away from the Feuler's cloak.

The soldier standing in the rear reached for his intercom. But before he could relay the message, the Feuler popped up behind him, fully reunited.

He chopped quick -*Shzz!* - severing the merc's head from his body.

The vanquishing slice shook the soldiers as they turned simultaneously.

And there the butcher stood, holding his giant knives.

The mercs opened fire as the Feuler split in half again, ducking the vicious lasers.

FL stood beside one merc, juggling his knife into the air.

As the merc turned to shoot, his hands fell from his body.

FL thrust his knife into the merc's stomach.

Shlp!

And with an up and down motion, he cut savagely across until the blade cut all the way through.

At the same time, FR slid behind the other mercenary. With a flick of his wrist, he aimed the butchering blade up, and —

Chup!

"Aaaghhhhh!!" the merc wailed as FR chopped deep between his legs.

The Feuler pushed and pulled in an upward-sawing motion.

Yanking his knife out of the man's chest cavity, he twirled the blade down, sloshing blood over the monorail windows.

Both of the Xaris soldiers fell apart into a splash of gore.

An instant death…

As it should be.

For the Feuler's knives cut before greeting a surface.

The Feuler rejoined, sheathing his mighty butcher knives in the rear of his utility belt.

The oily gore coated him fast as he collected a few organs.

Carrying the gobbets in his arms like gentle perishables, he strolled casually up to the railcar's entrance.

The men on the platform glared as the doors opened.

And there the Feuler stood, in the doorway, with no emotion. For a moment, he gazed lifelessly into the army of Xarchanzians.

Then he dumped the mutilated lumps onto the platform.

And with that same disturbing face…

The Feuler took a step back, and the monorail doors shut with haste, closing the mad slug up inside.

www.ingramcontent.com/pod-product-compliance
Lightning Source LLC
Chambersburg PA
CBHW010749310726
48980CB00003B/370
* 9 7 8 0 5 7 8 9 4 1 8 9 9 *